THE MOTOR HOME
WAS GONE!

We stood there staring with our mouths open.

"I don't believe it," Mr. Clappers said. "Who on earth could have taken it?"

I'd seen J.P. pick locks. It wouldn't have taken long—maybe fifteen minutes, and another fifteen minutes to cross the wires in the ignition system so they could start the engine. I'd seen J.P. do that too.

I felt terrible—sick and weak and ashamed . . .

Other Avon Flare Books by
James Lincoln Collier

THE WINCHESTERS

OUTSIDE
LOOKING
IN

JAMES LINCOLN COLLIER

AN AVON  FLARE BOOK

For Christopher and Julia

AVON BOOKS
A division of
The Hearst Corporation
105 Madison Avenue
New York, New York 10016

Copyright © 1987 by James Lincoln Collier
Published by arrangement with Macmillan Publishing Company
Library of Congress Catalog Card Number: 86-21845
ISBN: 0-380-70961-9
RL: 4.7

First Avon Flare Printing: September 1990

AVON FLARE TRADEMARK REG. U.S. PAT. OFF. AND IN OTHER COUNTRIES,
MARCA REGISTRADA, HECHO EN U.S.A.

Printed in the U.S.A.

RA 10 9 8 7 6 5 4 3 2 1

ONE

OOMA WAS GOING to steal the Walkman out of the baby's stroller as soon as she got the chance. There was a baby in the stroller, all bundled up in a pink blanket even though it was spring already and pretty warm. The Walkman was tucked down in the blanket next to the baby. The mother wasn't paying much attention to it. She was too interested in listening to J. P. make his sales talk about our amulets with the ancient Indian good-luck sign, the honey that lowered your blood pressure, and the pamphlet that J. P. had written called "Extracts from the Journals of J. P. Wheeler."

J. P. was kind of fat and had a big, brown mustache. "You know what causes high blood pressure, don't you, folks?" he asked. "It's problems with blood sugar. Medical science has proved that. Ask your doctor, if you don't believe me." He picked up a jar of honey. "Now, what's the answer to that?"

I'd heard it a thousand times, and I shut it off. Ooma had got her hand above her eyes like a sunshield and was looking up in the sky. In a couple of seconds, she sort of strolled over close to the stroller, like she was trying to get a better look at whatever it was up in the sky.

"Ooma," I said in a low voice, "I know what you're thinking about. Keep your hands off it."

She went on staring up into the sky with her hand above her eyes. "None of your damn business, Fergy," she replied under her breath. Ooma swore as well as stole.

"Yes, it is. You'll get us all in trouble again."

"Shut up," she said. "You can't tell me what to do."

We had got our folding table set up in front of a supermarket in a shopping mall somewhere in New Jersey. It was the usual shopping mall: a whole bunch of stores going in a big semicircle around a huge parking lot filled with cars. There were lots of people going in all directions, and about twenty or thirty were crowding around our folding table. When we set up anywhere, the first thing was for Ooma and me to get out our guitars and play and sing two or three numbers, and do this little dance we had, to draw a crowd. After that, we didn't have much to do except stand around. I looked at the woman with the stroller. She was wearing a scarf tied over her head, and she was pretty interested in what J. P. was saying. Ooma edged over toward her another couple of feet, still staring off into space. Now she was right next to the stroller.

I went after her. "I'll punch you, Ooma," I whispered. She was eight and I was fourteen, so I could punch her pretty much when I wanted to, except when J. P. or Gussie was looking.

"Mind your own damn business, Fergy." Now she bent over and started to scratch her leg. In a minute she would kneel down to scratch better, and two seconds later the Walkman would be out of the stroller.

"You better not," I whispered.

"Get the hell away from me, Fergy."

"Ooma—"

But then I heard a man's voice shout, "I'm sorry, you can't do that here, this is private property, you'll have to move on."

I looked around. A fat, bald guy in a tan cardigan

sweater was pushing through the crowd to the folding table with its amulets, pamphlets, and jars of honey. He got up to J. P. and clapped his hands. "Sorry, folks," he said. "This is private property. You can't sell here without a vendor's license."

It always happened. He would be the manager from the supermarket, or some security chief for the shopping mall, or somebody like that. J. P. liked it when they came after him, because he knew he was going to end up making the guy sore. He smiled and rubbed his hands together. "I'm sorry, sir," he said. "But we're exercising our constitutional right to practice our religion. We're a church, and you can't prevent us from exercising our freedom to worship in a public place." I took a couple of steps over to hear better.

The store manager put his hands on his hips. "You're a religion? Who're you trying to kid? You're peddling junk on private property and you can't do that."

J. P. went on smiling. "I'm sorry to have to contradict you," he said, "but this is a public thoroughfare, and you can't prevent us from practicing our religion here. Now, if you'll stand back so these good people can see, we won't take any more of your time. I'm sure you're a busy man and have a lot of things to do."

"Why, you half-baked pepperhead—"

Suddenly, I remembered Ooma, and I turned to her again. She was kneeling by the stroller, scratching her ankle. I looked back at J. P., trying to figure what to do. He was waving his hand in front of the store manager. "No insults, please. That's slander and we might be tempted to sue. In fact, if you interfere with our religious rights any further, I'll be forced to call the police." To be honest, I never really did understand how it worked about the religious rights. We were a church, all right; J. P. had a certificate from somebody saying that he was a minister. All I knew about the rest

3

of it was that J. P. said he'd talked it over with a lawyer and that we were within our rights.

"Call the police?" the store manager said. His face was red right across his bald head. "You bet I'm going to call the police."

He turned to stomp away when there was a shriek, and a woman's voice shouted, "That little girl stole my Walkman. She stole it right out of the stroller. I saw her—I saw her do it."

I whirled around, and so did J. P. and so did the store manager. The crowd was now all looking at Ooma and the woman. "I didn't do anything," Ooma shouted. "She's making it up." We were always getting into these messes, and I hated it. I hated seeing J. P. lie and squirm to get out of it. Who likes to see his own dad having to squirm all the time?

The store manager jumped over to Ooma and so did J. P. The woman pointed at Ooma. "She's got it under her dress. I saw her."

"I didn't take anything," Ooma said. It was her old trick, because mostly people wouldn't dare pull up her dress. In fact, a lot of people didn't like even to touch her, because of the dirt.

J. P. put his arm around her. "Ma'am," he said, "I know my little girl pretty well, and I'll give you my solemn word I've never known her to steal. She has her faults, but stealing isn't one of them."

The woman went on pointing to Ooma's skirt. Ooma used to wear jeans like the rest of us, but jeans made stealing too easy. She would go into a store and stand by the checkout counter pretending she was reading *People* or the *National Enquirer*, which was all a lie, because she could hardly read. And three minutes later, the front of her jeans would be full of Pezes and Life-savers and Clark Bars. I never could believe how she did it. One minute there'd be a Clark Bar on the rack and the next minute it would be gone and Ooma would be tucking in her shirt like it had come loose. So, finally, Gussie took her jeans away and made her wear a dress, but it didn't make much difference. We'd get back to the van we lived in and Ooma would go off in a corner by herself; and after a while we'd notice a big smear of chocolate by the corner of her mouth.

The manager knelt down in front of Ooma. "Now, little girl, give me that Walkman."

"I didn't steal anything," Ooma said.

"What nerve," the woman shouted.

The crowd was gathering around. J. P. said, "Ooma, you're not supposed to be walking around with that bad foot, anyway. I'll have to carry you back to the van." There wasn't anything wrong with Ooma's foot. J. P. knew that if she tried to walk with that Walkman between her legs she was going to look pretty funny. Besides, it might drop out. He started to bend down to pick her up, but before he could the manager grabbed her arm.

"Take your hands off that child before I have you arrested," J. P. said.

The manager let go. But then he grabbed Ooma by her shoulders, lifted her clear off the ground, and give her a shake. The Walkman dropped onto the pavement. The woman dove for it and snatched it up. "It's broken," she shouted. "Look, the case is cracked." She held it out for the crowd to see. "I just bought it two days ago. It cost thirty dollars. What I want to know is, Who's going to pay for it? That's what I want to know." She waved it toward J. P.

J. P. stood there with his hands on his hips. He puffed out his cheeks, blew out some air, then tugged on one end of his mustache. Finally, he reached into his pocket, took out his old worn-out wallet, counted out thirty dollars, and gave them to the woman.

"And now," the store manager said, "you and your church better get out of here before I call the cops." He turned and walked back into the store, and we began to pack up the stuff and load it back into the vans.

It seemed things like that were happening all the time, and I was sick and tired of it. Once the cops arrested J. P. for false advertising, because he couldn't prove that honey was good for your blood pressure. J. P. had to get a lawyer and go to court, and in the end he got fined a thousand dollars. He couldn't pay it, so they took one of the vans and all six of us had to live in the other one until J. P. and the Wiz reclaimed one from behind a grocery store one night. Another time, Ooma stole a bike off somebody's front porch. She didn't know how to ride it, because we'd never had bikes, and she rode it out in front of a car and got hit. She had to go into the hospital, and they wouldn't let her out until we could pay the bill. Finally, Gussie had to get a job at a checkout counter in a five-and-ten and J. P. had to go to work pumping gas to raise the money. We paid off half of it, got Ooma out, took off for the South, and couldn't ever come back to that town again.

Things like that were always happening to us. I hated it. Oh, how I wished we were a normal family. Oh, how I wished we lived in a regular house and I could go to school, and join the Boy Scouts, and be on some team, and play an instrument in the band. It didn't matter to me what kind of team, or what instrument, just so long as the whole thing was regular and normal.

The worst part of it was not going to school. I knew I was way behind most other kids—and falling further behind every day. Here I was, fourteen years old, and I didn't know the times table right and couldn't do long division, much less square roots or anything like that; and didn't know what chlorophyll was or how trees grew or what made electricity; and didn't know what the Constitution said, even though J. P. was always going on about our constitutional rights; and didn't know who'd fought in the Civil War, or why. I didn't know anything, except geography. I knew that, all right, because we'd been in every state except Alaska and Hawaii. We always had a lot of maps, which J. P. and the Wiz would reclaim from gas stations, and riding around in the van I had lots of time to study them. I knew all the capitals, even the hard ones like Frankfort, Kentucky, and Springfield, Illinois. But geography was all I knew; I didn't know anything else.

I'd only gone to school twice in my life. The first time was when we lived on the old commune with a bunch of people like ourselves. There wasn't much to do around that place in the winter, and so the grownups decided to have a school for us kids. The thing of it was, though, everybody on the commune was supposed to do his own thing. There weren't supposed to be any rules about anything. Anybody who wanted to give us a course could teach anything he wanted. One person gave us wildflowers and another one gave us sex education and another gave us motorcycle maintenance. I was only around seven then, and for a long time afterward I thought that was what school was—where everybody sat around on the floor as close to the wood stove as they could get and listened to some grown-up give us a long talk about something.

The second time I went to school I learned better. It was the time that J. P. had got put into jail for false advertising about the honey. We were stuck in that town for a couple of months, so the cops came around and said I had to go to school. Ooma was only four and went to kindergarten, but I was ten. They tested me and found out that I didn't know anything about anything. I could hardly read or write, and could add and subtract only a little and didn't know the times tables past three times three. They put me in the second grade, and I sat all scrunched up in a desk half my size, coloring in pictures of hens and the Cookie Monster in a workbook. Oh, it made me miserable, all right. The teacher would call on me to read, and I'd stumble around and bumble around, feeling all hot and sweaty, until she'd give it to some seven-year-old who'd whiz right through it.

Oh, I tell you, I hated being dumber than a bunch of seven-year-olds. I used to get revenge when we went out for recess and played soccer, because I was twice as big as they were and could get the ball away from them whenever I wanted. It cheered me up a lot when I did that, because after a while they would get mad and sulk.

But, to tell the truth, I wasn't really much good at sports, either. How can you practice baseball or soccer when you live in a van and never settle down anyplace? When we lived on the commune with all those people like us, the grown-ups played Frisbee a lot when they ought to have been cutting wood for the winter. We were up there for three winters and ran out of wood in the middle of January all three times, so us kids spent most of our time out in the snow carrying wood back to the house, a log at a time. It made us good and sore because it burned up nearly as fast as we could carry it in. We never got to sit by the fire ourselves until our clothes were soaked and we were sneezing and shivering and the little ones were crying. Anyway, they played a lot of Frisbee on that commune, and so I got good at that. In December and January, before the wood ran out, they used to get up skating parties and I got good at that, too. At least, I got good at skating, but I didn't learn how to play hockey, because hockey was competitive and we weren't allowed to play competitive games. We were supposed to be a peaceful and loving community, which was a big lie, because the kids were always fighting and the grown-ups were always arguing about whose turn it was to chop wood and whose turn it was to sit in front of the fire and drink wine. I noticed that there never was any shortage of money for wine on that commune.

Anyway, the third time we ran out of wood, everybody sort of gave up, and that's when J. P. and the Wiz took the vans from the commune and we made up our church. It wasn't stealing, J. P. said; He and the Wiz always did most of the work around there, and the commune owed them something.

Anyway, I never got to practice competitive games very much, but I was better at soccer than those second-graders, and I could get some revenge on them. It helped a little, but not very much. Oh, it was terrible being scrunched up in one of those little desks, and after about four days of it I got bound and determined to learn how to read and write and spell and multiply and divide. I was falling further and further behind every day. And it scared the pants off me that when I grew up I'd be as dumb as a second-grader. Then what would happen to me? I wouldn't be able to get any kind of a job at all and would have to spend the rest of my life riding around in a beat-up old van selling good-luck amulets and honey that was supposed to cure high blood pressure, and handing out "Extracts from the Journals of J. P. Wheeler."

So, during the time I was going to school there while J. P. was in jail, I worked as hard as I could on my reading and arithmetic, and toward the end, they put me into the third grade. That was a big thing for me, to be promoted like that. It was a thrill, and I realized that if I stuck at it and worked hard, I'd get into the fourth grade pretty soon. But then the court case got over, J. P. got out of jail, and we left that town. Naturally, I began begging Gussie and J. P. to get me some arithmetic books and fourth-grade readers and so forth. J. P. was

9

all against it. He said, "Those books are filled with materialism. You think it's just about Dick and Jane and Spot and Tim, but you'll notice how everybody has a big house and cars and television sets. Right along with the spelling you're getting the whole materialistic philosophy of life. They start sticking it to kids in the first grade."

Gussie said, "J. P., you're always sticking your philosophy at them. What's the difference?"

"The difference is that I'm not using my philosophy to exploit them. I'm using it to show them how the system is set up to sell them a bill of goods—get them to want things and then force them into working for the system to pay for them." That was why we couldn't call them Mom and Dad, but had to call them J. P. and Gussie. J. P. always said, " 'Dad' implies a power relationship, and I'm not into power."

"Still," Gussie said, "I don't see what the harm is in learning to read and write." Sometimes I got the feeling that Gussie didn't exactly believe in all of J. P.'s ideas. So she got us some readers. Ooma scaled hers off into the woods once when we were camping, but I went to work on mine. After a while, I could read pretty good, and add and subtract, and do most of the times tables, except ones like eight times seven and nine times eight. But that was about all I knew. Oh, how I wanted to be normal and live in a house and go to school. I knew that was wrong; I knew that was materialism; and it made me feel guilty for wanting it. But I wanted it all the same.

TWO

AFTER THE TROUBLE we had over Ooma trying to steal the Walkman, J. P. got afraid word would get around that part of New Jersey, and shopping-mall security people would be on the lookout for us. So, the next morning J. P. decided we should head for New York City.

There was good money to be made in New York, J. P. always said. The place was full of tourists who were short on brains and had plenty of money to spend.

"How do you know they're short on brains?" I said.

"They wouldn't be in New York if they had any," J. P. said.

"How come they have so much money if they don't have brains?" I said.

"Fergy, in the United States of America it takes brains to avoid having money."

"Then how come there are so many poor people you're always talking about?"

"That's the point," J. P. said. "In a materialistic society where everybody is scrambling for money, some people are bound to get left out. It's like musical chairs—there isn't any point in the game if there's a chair for everybody, is there? The idea is not for everybody to have enough money, but for some people to have more money than others so you can tell who won and who lost."

The whole subject confused me. The truth was, I

wished we had more money instead of being broke all the time. I wished we had at least enough money to buy a big motor home, with a kitchen and bunks and so forth. When we would stay at federal campsites, which were cheap, we would see these terrific motor homes. Some of them even had television sets and toilets in them. I would have liked having a toilet. We were always having to find gas stations so we could go to the bathroom, and at night, when we were sleeping in the van, we had to get up and go outside. J. P. was right about materialism; I could see that. But I still wished we had more money. I couldn't help it; that was just the way I felt.

We headed for New York. I sat by the rear window of the van. It was around eight o'clock in the morning, and every once in a while we would go through some suburban town and pass a school. The kids were all going along the sidewalk in bunches, talking and fooling around and punching each other. They were dressed up nice, too—nice sweaters or jackets, good jeans, and new shoes. What did it feel like to be one of them, I wondered. It seemed to me that it must be a whole lot of fun to be going along like that with a bunch of other kids, just fooling around. Once we passed some kids from some kind of private school. They were wearing shirts and ties and jackets with emblems on their breast pockets. Oh, how I wished I had a jacket with an emblem on the breast pocket.

Then I realized that Ooma was scratching herself. "Ooma's scratching again," I said.

"I am not," she said. "I'm just itching."

"Yes, you are," I said. "She's going to get that skin disease again."

Gussie was sitting up in the front seat next to J. P. "Come here, Ooma," she said. Ooma crawled up to the front. Gussie lifted up Ooma's shirt and looked. "I don't see anything," she said.

"You worry about things too much, Fergy," J. P. said. "You've got to go with the flow more."

I wished he wouldn't say things like that. Ooma was always getting some kind of skin disease, and then she'd scratch all night and keep everybody awake. "She's dirty," I said. "She needs a bath."

"Mind your own damn business, Fergy," Ooma said.

"A little dirt never hurt anybody," J. P. said. "From earth we come, to earth we go. Dirt is mankind's natural element."

"Well, she's going to get that skin disease again if she doesn't have a bath."

"Stop worrying about it, Fergy," J. P. said.

But Gussie said, "There's no point in taking a chance. We'll go to a Y when we get to New York and all have showers."

"You're beginning to sound like a camp director, Gussie," J. P. said.

"You're not the final authority on everything, J. P.," Gussie said. "I know a few things."

J. P. gave her a quick look and then turned back to the road. "You've been getting pretty snappish recently," he said.

Gussie looked straight ahead out the windshield down the road. "Maybe it's about time I started doing a little thinking for myself," she said.

"Maybe it's about time you got yourself into a better frame of mind," J. P. said.

Now she looked at him. "Maybe it's your frame of mind that needs improving," she said.

He didn't say anything and they dropped it. The whole thing kind of surprised me. It wasn't like Gussie to contradict J. P. He was supposed to be the great man and know everything about everything. I gave Ooma a little look to see what she thought of it. She was kind of staring at Gussie with her thumb in her mouth. I could tell she was surprised by it, too.

At about ten o'clock, we drove across the George Washington Bridge into New York City. I always liked that part. The bridge was way up high, and as you drove across it you could see little boats down below— sailboats, tugboats pulling barges, sometimes big ocean cruisers. And way downriver you could see the towers of the World Trade Center and a whole lot of other tall buildings I didn't know the names of. It was a nice view, and I liked looking at it.

Then we came off the bridge and headed down the West Side Highway. You weren't supposed to drive on the West Side Highway in a van, but J. P. didn't worry too much about obeying laws. He drove wherever he wanted to and parked wherever he wanted to, and he threw away the parking tickets he got. About every six months we changed the registration to a different state— Pennsylvania, Ohio, Florida, Missouri —wherever we happened to be. We moved around an awful lot and it was pretty hard for them to catch up with us.

So we went down the West Side Highway, on across to SoHo, and parked the vans in an illegal place on a side street, just off West Broadway. SoHo was a part of New York where they had a lot of painters and sculptors and writers. The buildings weren't much to look at— just dirty brick buildings mostly five or six stories high, with old, iron fire escapes along the fronts. But in the bottom floors of most of them were art galleries filled with weird paintings, fancy restaurants with trees in the middle of them, and shops selling used blue jeans for a hundred dollars a pair. "There's plenty of money in SoHo," J. P. always said. "Besides, it's full of tourists."

We carried the folding table around the corner onto West Broadway and set it up. In New York, they mostly didn't bother you about selling things on the street; the place was full of street sellers. But it was different from working a shopping mall, where there was always a lot of room to set up. On West Broadway, we had to put the folding table as close to the wall as we could, so there'd be room for a good-sized crowd on the sidewalk in front of it. The Wiz and I set the table up, and the others began bringing out boxes of amulets and honey.

The Wiz was a tall, skinny black guy who wore glasses. They called him the Wiz because he had been to about six different colleges and had studied everything there was to study and was very philosophical about everything. He was especially hot on a writer called Henry David Thoreau, who had gone off to live all alone in a hut by a lake and think deep thoughts. The Wiz had all of Henry Thoreau's books in a little book rack on the wall of the other van, where he lived with a woman named Trotsky. The Wiz believed in civil disobedience and liked breaking laws he disagreed with and getting thrown in jail for it. "Well, Fergy," he said as we were setting up the folding table, "here we are among the manswarm again." The Wiz could never say it was pretty crowded or there were a lot of people around. He had to say it was the "manswarm" or something philosophical like that.

"I wish I could study philosophy," I said.

"Perhaps someday that will be a feasible course of action, Fergy."

I shook my head. "If I can't even do long division, how can I study philosophy?"

He looked at me. "J. P.'s correct, Fergy. The public-school system is there primarily to inculcate materialistic values in order that the wealthy may stay wealthy and the impoverished stay poor."

I didn't want to hear any more of that for a while, so

I dropped the subject. Ooma and I got out our guitars and went into our usual routine to collect a crowd. J. P. had worked the routine out to include a little of everything, so as to attract the widest possible crowd. First, we did some new disco hit and then a Beatles tune like "I Wanna Hold Your Hand"—the crowd always thought it was cute when Ooma pranced around and sang that, while I played the guitar. Then we would do a folk song like "On Top of Old Smokey" for the folk-music fans, and a jazz tune like "When the Saints Go Marching In" for the jazz fans, and finally I would do a little bit of a Bach cantata that J. P. had made me learn, for the classical-music fans. The whole show took about fifteen minutes, and by the time we finished we usually had a pretty good-sized crowd—thirty, forty people—and J. P. would go into his sales talk.

So we did our routine, and J. P. started talking, and I blanked my mind out and started daydreaming about going to college like the Wiz and studying so hard, day and night, that I became the smartest man in the world. I'd just got around to the part where the president was calling me down to Washington to ask my advice on the economic situation when I noticed that Ooma was gone. I looked over at the folding table. J. P. was holding up a jar of honey and saying, "Don't take my word for it, ask your doctor." Gussie and Trotsky were selling things and making change, and the Wiz was going through the crowd handing out copies of "Extracts from the Journals of J. P. Wheeler." None of them had noticed that Ooma was gone. I took a quick look up the street. There was a restaurant there, and beyond that an art gallery. I didn't figure Ooma would go into either of those. Across West Broadway was another art gallery, a fancy dress store, and a store that sold quilts and dolls and stuff. It didn't figure that Ooma would go into any of those, either. So I darted on up the street, stopping to look into each store through the window, just in case. I didn't see Ooma anywhere. I crossed West Broadway and came down that side, still looking in stores. But I didn't see her.

Then I heard the sound of a cop siren, sort of low. I looked down the street. A cop car was pulling up to the curb, its lights flashing, the siren making a dying hum. I ran on down there, ducking and dodging around the people and praying it wouldn't be Ooma they were after. I came up to the cop car. The cops were just getting out, and a few people had stopped on the sidewalk to watch. Then the cops marched into a kind of fancy food store that had in the window pastries and jellies and meat loaves with sausages in them. I dashed up to the window and looked in. A woman in a white apron had hold of Ooma by the back of her shirt. Ooma was wriggling around, but when she saw the cops come marching in, she stopped wriggling and looked plenty scared. I was pretty scared, too: If all she'd stolen was a few cookies or something, they probably wouldn't have called the cops.

One of the cops crouched down in front of her and started to talk to her. She stuck her thumb in her mouth and stood there nodding and shaking her head to the cop's questions. Then the cop stood up and patted her on the shoulder, and they came on out of there, first one cop, then Ooma, and then the other cop. Were they going to let her go? It was going to be one more terrible mess if they didn't, and I knew I'd get the blame for it.

Out they came onto the sidewalk. They marched Ooma up to the cop car, opened the back door, and put her in. Then they went around to their own doors.

What should I do? I knew it wasn't smart for us to mess around with cops—cops were always trouble for us. But I couldn't let my own sister be hauled off that way. I ran up to the cop car and looked in the window.

"That's my sister," I said. "She doesn't mean to be bad. She can't help herself."

The cop gave me a squinty look. "Your sister? Where do you live?"

There wasn't any good answer to that. J. P. sure wouldn't want me bringing cops around, because about half of what we did was illegal one way or another—sleeping in vans was illegal because you didn't have toilets and running water; selling stuff on the streets was illegal, even though everybody did it; and besides, our vans were illegally parked. "I'll go get J—my dad," I said.

I started off, but the cop grabbed my arm before I could take more than a step. "No, you don't, sonny," he said. "You hop in back and we'll help you find him."

There wasn't anything to do, so I got in the back with Ooma. "What did you do this time?" I whispered.

"None of your damn business," she whispered.

I shut my mouth, and the cops drove up West Broadway. I pointed out the place where Gussie and J. P. and the rest were selling amulets and honey and giving away J. P.'s pamphlets. "That's them," I said.

"It figures," one of the cops said. They stopped the car. We all got out, and the cops sort of pushed us ahead of them through the crowd. When we came out to the front, J. P. was saying, "Five centuries ago the Indians living right on this spot, Manhattan Island, discovered a talisman that could bring the bearer good luck. Today—" Then he saw us.

The cops pushed us up to the folding table. "These your brats?"

J. P. looked down at us. I could tell that he was thinking of saying he'd never seen us before. But he knew Gussie wouldn't have allowed that. "What's this

18

all about, Fergy?'' he said. "I thought I could trust you, at least."

"I didn't do anything," I said. "Ooma did something. I was looking for her so I could stop her."

The cop pointed to Ooma. "The girl stole a hundred bucks out of a cash register in a store down the block. The other kid was waiting outside for her to come out."

I was pretty shocked. A hundred bucks was an awful lot. "I wasn't in on it," I said. "I just went looking for her."

The cop who was doing the talking didn't pay any attention to me. "Where do you folks live?" The crowd was hanging around to watch. I felt embarrassed.

"We're a religious organization," J. P. said. He grabbed up a pamphlet. "Here," he said, handing it to the cop. "It contains our spiritual message. We have a mission to bring a message of understanding to the world."

The cop turned the pamphlet over in his hand, but he didn't open it up to look at the spiritual message. "Okay, you're a religious organization. Where do you live?"

J. P. was beginning to sweat on his forehead. He pulled at one end of his mustache. "We live upstate," he said.

"In New York City—where are you staying in New York City?"

J. P. wiped a little sweat off his forehead. "Officer, I admit I'm nonplussed. I can't imagine my little girl stealing anything, let alone a large sum of money. She has her faults, but stealing is not one of them. Of course, she's high-spirited, and sometimes she gets up to mischief—"

"I asked you where you're staying."

"Oh, we won't be staying. We're leaving soon."

"You may be staying longer than you think. How do you cart this stuff around—got a truck or something?"

19

There wasn't any way out of it. "We've got a couple of vans," J. P. said.

"Where?"

J. P. pointed. "Around the corner."

The cop jerked his head in that direction. "Frank, go have a look," he said.

The other cop went around the corner. In about two minutes he was back. "They're gypsies," he said. "They got a camp stove in there, a big plastic orange cooler, and sleeping bags." He looked at J. P. "You're illegal about six different ways," he said. He turned to the other cop. "What do you want to do with them?"

"The woman in the store said she doesn't want to press charges since she got her money back," said the first cop. He turned to J. P. "Okay, buddy," he said. "You just pile your religious organization into those vans and head on out of this city. The next time, we're going to take you in."

THREE

THERE WASN'T ANYTHING to do but drive back out to New Jersey. We crossed over the George Washington Bridge again, and I sat looking out the rear window at the river far below and the huge buildings down at the bottom end of Manhattan, looming up in the sunlight, solid as steel and big as mountains.

J. P. was furious at Ooma. "Don't you have any sense, Ooma?" he shouted at her.

"Don't blame me," she said. "I didn't think they were looking."

"You've caused the family a lot of trouble in the past few days, Ooma," he shouted.

Ooma stuck out her lip. "It wasn't my fault. I didn't think they were looking."

"Well, you better be sure next time," J. P. shouted.

Tears began to roll out of Ooma's eyes and down her cheeks, leaving white tracks in the dirt. "Don't keep blaming me," she said.

Suddenly Gussie said, "Leave her alone, J. P."

J. P. swung his head around to give Gussie a quick look. "What?" he said.

"Stop shouting at her," Gussie said. "Where do you think she picks up those ideas?"

"You stay out of this, Gussie," J. P. snapped.

She gave him a look. "No, I won't stay out of it. She's my child, too."

J. P. frowned. He wasn't used to Gussie standing up

to him this way, and he didn't know what to make of it. "Let's save this for later, Gussie," he said. "I'm dealing with Ooma right now."

I was sick of the whole thing and decided to tune out my brain so I wouldn't hear the argument. More and more, I was beginning to think that I didn't belong with the rest of them. I didn't fit in. They had their beliefs and that was fine, for they were entitled to them: J. P. was a great man and had wonderful ideas, and one day his journals would be famous. But I was having an awful lot of trouble believing in his ideas. I knew it was my fault. Probably if I tried harder I could get myself to believe in them. Lots of times, maybe when I was trying to go to sleep, I'd go over his ideas, like there shouldn't be any power in the world, and everybody should be equal, and governments should be abolished, and all the rest of it. They sounded like good ideas: What could be wrong with ideas like that? But all the time I was trying to believe in them, contrary ideas kept creeping into my mind, like would people really be good by their own natural selves if there wasn't any government? I mean, look at Ooma. She was allowed to do anything she wanted, and instead of being good and kind she was just as wild as she could be. Were we really entitled to reclaim anything we wanted because the system had stolen it from us in the first place? Take that Walkman Ooma tried to steal from that stroller. Did it really belong to the system or to that woman?

Oh, I knew I had to be wrong about it. Gussie and the Wiz and Trotsky all believed in J. P.'s ideas and said that one day his journals would be famous. I mean, if the Wiz believed in them, they must be so, because he'd been to all those colleges and had studied everything. But try as I might to believe, I couldn't. And it was beginning to seem to me that maybe the best thing for everybody would be for me to leave.

22

But, when I thought of getting out of my own family, I got scared. Where would I go? How would I live? If I was going to school the way I wanted, I'd have to live in some kind of a regular home and all of that. I didn't know anybody who lived in a regular home. It was a problem, all right.

We got out to New Jersey, found a shopping mall in some town, and worked it for a while. Ooma was still feeling grumpy. She wouldn't put any effort into our songs, wouldn't sing "I Wanna Hold Your Hand," and messed up the chord changes so it all sounded pretty bad. We had a late start, too, so between everything we ended up making twelve bucks, which gave us a total of twenty-nine. Out of that we had to buy gas for the vans. There wasn't much left for lunch, so we ate peanut-butter sandwiches and drank Coke in the backs of the vans, right there in the shopping mall. Everybody was feeling kind of gloomy about it. J. P. and the Wiz talked over reclaiming some tuna fish and cheese from the supermarket in the shopping mall, so as to give us a more balanced diet. After all, J. P. said, it was a free country and a person had a right to give his family a balanced diet. But they decided against it: Our luck wasn't running very well, and it didn't seem like a good time to take chances.

Then a cop came along and told us we couldn't camp in the shopping mall. So we got into the vans and wasted a lot of gas driving out into the country where we could park on a back road alongside a patch of woods. And that was when I decided I would talk to J. P. about the whole thing.

"All right, Fergy," he said. "Let's take a walk."

It was getting on toward five o'clock by now. The sky had clouded over, and it was a little chilly. We walked on down the road until the woods on one side gave out. There was a field there, with stone walls

23

around it, and down at the other side of the field a white clapboard house. In the field, a bunch of kids were playing with a football—a couple of girls and three or four guys—little ones, big ones. They weren't playing a game exactly, but were just running around and tossing the football back and forth among themselves and shouting and hollering, "Give it here." The house was just an ordinary house. A string of blue gray wood smoke was coming out of the chimney. Even at that distance I could smell the smoke. After a while the kids would go inside, at least the ones who lived there. They would warm up in front of the fire, and then they would wash their hands and faces and go into the dining room and eat their suppers. Maybe they would have fried chicken, peas, and mashed potatoes and gravy, although maybe they weren't that rich and would only have hot dogs and baked beans. But I hoped it would be fried chicken and mashed potatoes—I loved mashed potatoes with gravy on them.

We sat down on the stone wall where we could watch the kids toss the football around. "Look at that, Fergy," J. P. said. "Competition. It's just training for war."

"They just seem to be tossing the ball around," I said.

J. P. shrugged. "It comes down to the same thing. So. What's on your mind, Fergy?"

I swallowed, because it isn't easy to tell your own dad what he ought to do. "J. P., maybe if we had a regular house, and you and Gussie had regular jobs, and Ooma and I went to school, maybe Ooma wouldn't be getting into trouble all the time."

J. P. turned his head to look at me. He just looked for a while, tugging at his mustache. "Where'd you get a strange idea like that from, Fergy? Who've you been talking to?"

"Nobody," I said. "It's my own idea. I didn't get it from anybody."

He didn't say anything for a minute. I sat on the stone wall, smelling the wood smoke and watching the kids play. One of the big kids had the football and was dodging around while the others chased him. Finally, they got him down and piled on top of him. "Fergy," J. P. said, "it's pretty disappointing for me to hear you say something like that. I thought I'd taught you better. Don't you realize what the system will do to you if it hooks you?"

I knew, because he'd told us often enough. "Well, I know, J. P. They'll turn me into one of their automatons. They'll lure me in with material goods and then trap me into spending the rest of my life manufacturing instant obsolescence and the tools of war."

"Exactly," J. P. said. Out in the field, a couple of girls had got the football away from the big kid and were racing around, passing it to each other to keep it away from the rest. "First, they lure you in with something small—a Walkman, something like that. So you go to work for them to pay for it in a deadly, monotonous factory somewhere, pushing a button or pulling a lever a thousand times an hour. Then, they get your mouth watering for something bigger—a new car, maybe. So you tell yourself you'll work for them a little longer—what's the difference if you put in a couple of more years? The next thing you know, you've got a credit card, a revolving charge account, you're up to here in debt, and they've got you, because you have to keep on working for them until you get the debt cleared off. And you never will, because they'll keep on luring you in with more goodies—a house in the suburbs, a swimming pool, a vacation condo in Florida. The next thing you know, you're retired and you've spent your whole life working for a company that makes nuclear weapons or cars designed to fall apart in three years, or planning TV advertisements meant to sell the system to the next generation coming along. You know all this, Fergy. It's all in the journals. Haven't I explained it often enough?"

"Yes," I said. Out in the field, a couple of the little kids had got hold of the girl with the ball and were trying to tackle her. She threw it to the other girl, but it wasn't a good throw and the ball bounced along the ground. They all chased after it. "The only thing is, J. P., sometimes I have trouble believing it."

He gave me a long look and pulled at his mustache again. "Isn't it obvious to you, Fergy? Maybe you better go back and do some more reading in the journals."

I hoped he wouldn't make me do that. Even if he was my father, the journals were the most boring things I'd ever read, all full of philosophy and his ideas about the system and so forth. The only good parts were where he told stories about the bad things that the system did to us, such as arresting him for false advertising about the honey. Or the time that Ooma got some kind of contagious skin disease in Hartford and they put her in a home for a week until she got better. Or the time that J. P. and the Wiz got caught draining gas-pump hoses in a gas station late at night and had to go to jail overnight until we could earn enough money to get them out. Those parts of the journals were interesting, but most of it was J. P.'s thoughts and boring as could be.

"Well," I said, "I know you're right, but I'm having an awful lot of trouble believing it. I mean, what's better about telling people our honey cures high blood pressure than regular TV advertising?"

"It *is* good for hypertension," J. P. said. "I read it in a magazine somewhere."

Out in the field, the kids were all piled together like a bunch of puppies. The football was underneath them. "You always told us not to believe anything we read in magazines. You said it was all propaganda for the system."

He looked kind of cross, and I wished I hadn't said it. "It wasn't that kind of a magazine. It was a medical journal." He gave me a look. "You've got to understand, Fergy. The system is set up to steal from us; it's only fair for us to reclaim what we need."

I didn't say anything, just sat there on that stone wall looking out at the kids piled up in the field. A bell began to ring down near the clapboard house. The kids unpiled themselves and began to jog toward the house, still tossing the football back and forth among them. "J. P., I'm worried about not going to school. I'm getting dumber and dumber every day, and I'm scared that by the time I'm grown-up I won't know anything and it'll be too late."

He frowned and looked down at his hands. Then he looked at me and said, "Ninety percent of what you learn in school is propaganda, Fergy. What can you expect? They're paid by the system, so they teach the values of the system."

"Well, yes," I said. "But what about arithmetic and science and stuff like that? I can't even do long division."

"You can learn that stuff on your own, Fergy. Gussie can get you some books and help you."

I wasn't sure she could. Gussie's father was a professor of history at Harvard. His name was Gordon E. Hamilton, and his wife's name was Margaret Hamilton. They were our grandparents, but we hardly knew anything about them. J. P. didn't like Gussie to talk about them to us, and we weren't allowed to see them, because they tried to have J. P. put in jail when Gussie ran away with him when she was sixteen. But, sometimes, when Gussie was in the right mood and J. P. wasn't around, she would tell Ooma and me what it was like when she was our age. They had two servants—a cook and a maid to clean and serve the meals. They ate at a fancy table filled with silverware and glasses that cost

27

thousands of dollars. "We always had cut flowers on the table, flowers cut fresh every day. Oh, the table looked so beautiful when it was set, with the light from the chandelier glinting off the glasses and the silver so shiny and bright. I thought it was beautiful when I was a little girl. I was so proud of my parents for having such beautiful things. My dad was a famous historian, and important people were always coming to the house for dinner. My mother was beautiful. She was descended from Priscilla Alden and had played with Governor Waters and Senator Fillmore when they were children. My parents seemed so wonderful to me, like movie stars—sort of beautiful and faraway. I always knew I wasn't good enough for them. Then I met J. P. and he changed my life."

"How did you meet J. P.?"

"He came to Harvard to work on a demonstration against war. My father was on some committee, and J. P. came to our house to talk to him. I decided he was a great man and I fell in love, and when the administration broke up the demonstration, the police came after J. P. and we had to jump out of a window in Leveret House and get out of Cambridge. It seemed so romantic to me."

The police caught up with them, tried to put J. P. in jail for kidnapping Gussie, and brought Gussie home. But she ran away again, and, since she was over sixteen and was going with J. P. of her own free will, they couldn't do anything to J. P. And that was why we were never allowed to see our grandparents.

A lot of times I wondered what our grandparents were like. Were they nice? Were they funny or sad or what? Would they like me if we ever went to visit them? For I was determined that one day, when I was grown-up and didn't have to do what J. P. said anymore, I would go to visit them, if they weren't already dead.

28

But it meant that Gussie never had had any schooling after she was sixteen, so I didn't know how much she could teach me. She probably knew about long division and chlorophyll, but I figured that somebody who dropped out in the tenth grade couldn't be too good of a teacher. J. P. was older and had started college, but after a year he'd dropped out and hitchhiked all over the United States getting up demonstrations. He probably knew more than Gussie did, but I knew he wouldn't teach me, because he was always too busy writing his journals.

"J. P., I ought to go to a regular school, so I could be sure I was learning right."

J. P. slapped his knee, looking kind of exasperated. "Fergy, I think we've had enough of this conversation. I'm not going to go back on my principles just to suit you. We'll get you some books to study from." He got up from the stone wall and started back to where the vans were parked. I went on sitting there. Down at the end of the field, the kids were going into the white clapboard house, the whole bunch of them. I figured that the mother would give them all Cokes and cookies, unless she figured it would spoil their appetites for the fried chicken and the mashed potatoes and gravy.

FOUR

WE WORKED AROUND New Jersey for a while, mostly in shopping malls in the suburbs. "There's plenty of money in these places," J. P. said. "They're bored and they don't know what to do with it. You can sell these suckers anything if you pitch it right. Tell them it'll make people admire them, tell them it'll make them feel good, tell them it'll make them rich. The system's got them conditioned to believe that products will solve their problems. If you've got troubles, there's always something you can buy to relieve them."

That was one thing J. P. was right about. He told people that the amulets were mystic symbols invented by the Indians five hundred years ago right on that very spot of wherever we were, and they believed it and paid fifteen dollars apiece for them. He told them that the honey would cure high blood pressure and a whole lot of other things, too, and they believed that and paid fifteen dollars for that, too. He told them that the answers to their problems were all in the "Extracts from the Journals of J. P. Wheeler," and they took the pamphlets and read them looking for the answers. They probably would have read all the journals, not just the extracts, but the journals were hundreds of pages long— and getting longer all the time—and we couldn't afford to have them printed up. It was expensive enough getting a thirty-two-page pamphlet of extracts printed. Gussie always said we ought to sell them, instead of giving them away, but J. P. wouldn't hear of that. He wanted them to have the widest possible readership. "We're gaining thousands of adherents every year," he said. "We're whetting their appetites for the complete work. Someday we'll start printing that up volume by volume and sell it. It'll make a fortune."

But even if we weren't making any money on the pamphlets, we were doing okay with the amulets and the honey. We were going along pretty well, able to eat at McDonald's and Burger King and buy wine for the grown-ups. Then Ooma got us in trouble again. The way it happened was this: We were parked in a shopping mall, set up in front of a store called Madman Meyer's Electronic Cabin, which sold stereos and transistors and stuff like that. J. P. should have known better, for Ooma has a special weakness for radios and cassette players. The minute we finished our act and J. P. started his sales pitch about the honey, she went over to the window of Madman Meyer's and stood there with her thumb in her mouth looking at the stuff. I went over and stood next to her. "Ooma, just forget it," I said. "You're going to get us in trouble again. If you do, we'll be back to peanut-butter sandwiches and won't be able to eat at McDonald's anymore."

"I wasn't thinking anything," she said around her thumb.

"Yes, you were," I said. "Now, just forget it."

"I wasn't thinking."

Just then J. P. signaled me to bring him another case of honey from the van. I went over there, trying to keep an eye on Ooma as best I could. I climbed into the van, dragged out a carton of honey, and took another look at Ooma. She was still standing there in front of the window, with her thumb in her mouth. I brought the case over to the folding table, and then, as usual, the manager of Madman Meyer's came out of the store shouting at us. "Who gave you permission to do this?"

31

"The Constitution of the United States gave us permission," J. P. said, giving the manager a smile. "We're exercising our First Amendment rights. We're a religious organization."

The manager stood behind the folding table next to J. P., with his hands on his hips. "I don't care if you're Saint Alabaster the Great, you're blocking my door. Now, pack up and get out of here before I call the police."

J. P. gave the crowd a big wink and they laughed. "Please do call the police," he said. "They'll be pretty thrilled that you're interfering with our First Amendment rights."

"You can bet I'm going to interfere with your First Amendment rights. We'll see what the police have to say about it." He stomped off into his store.

I followed him a little bit to see what he would do. Sure enough, through the window I could see him go over to the phone hanging on the wall behind the counter and dial. Then I realized that Ooma wasn't there anymore. I spun around and saw her slipping into the back of the van, carrying a radio near as big as a bread box. I dashed over to the van and grabbed her by the shoulder. "Give me that thing," I said. I made a grab for it, and then I heard a shout. I looked back. The manager of Madman Meyer's was standing in front of the store, with his hands on his hips, looking quickly all around him. His mouth was grim, and I knew we were going to be in serious trouble the minute he found that radio. "Quick, Ooma. Shove that thing inside a sleeping bag."

Then I ran back over to J. P. "We better get out of here," I said in a low voice. "Ooma's got a huge, big radio in the van."

J. P. glanced at his watch. "I'm sorry, folks," he said in a loud voice. "I'm afraid our time's up. We're due in Metuchen in half an hour to deliver our spiritual

32

message to a group there." In a low voice he said to the others, "Ooma's done it again. Let's get out of here."

We began flinging the honey, amulets, and pamphlets back into their cartons. The manager came over to us. "Oh, no you don't," he snarled, grabbing onto J. P.'s arm. "The cops are on their way, and you're staying right here until they come. I'm going to have them make a search of those vans, and when they find that radio I'm going to see you locked up, the whole dirty bunch of you." The crowd stayed to see what would happen.

"Take your niquids off me, fella," J. P. said. He jerked loose, but the manager grabbed him again.

Now the Wiz stepped over. He was a good four inches taller than the manager and loomed over him. "You heard what the man said. Release that appendage from your clutch."

The manager looked up at the Wiz, let go of J. P., and backed away, trying to figure out what to do. Suddenly, he dashed forward and began dumping over the cardboard cartons. At the same moment we heard the faint whine of a police siren in the distance. "Let's get moving," J. P. shouted. The Wiz made a lunge at the manager, who ran back into the store. We threw all of our stuff into the boxes and heaved it into the vans helter-skelter, the pamphlets flying, the jars of honey rolling around the floor. Then we jumped into our van. J. P. started the engine and began to drive across the parking lot, with the other van coming along behind us.

The police siren was a lot louder now. There was a low wall of concrete barriers across the front of the parking lot, with a couple of openings in it marked EXIT and ENTRANCE. J. P. raced toward the exit. Now I could see two police cars speeding along the road outside the shopping mall toward the entrance. We tore up toward the exit. Suddenly, the first police car swung into it, braked hard, and skidded sideways, blocking the exit. "Damn," J. P. shouted. He swerved. The tires squealed, and then we rammed into the concrete barrier. I banged against the backseat and Ooma slid into me. The next thing I knew the hood was sprung up, there was a big crack in the windshield, and Gussie was holding her hand to her forehead.

The cops jumped out of their cars and ran toward us, unbuckling their holsters. "All of you, out," they shouted. We climbed out. They frisked J. P. and Gussie, and I stood there beside the van, looking at it. The radiator was mashed in against the engine, and the right front wheel was ripped out at a funny angle. It didn't look like we would ever drive that van again.

Now the manager of Madman Meyer's came running up, shouting about his radio. So the cops searched the van, while the manager kept bouncing around and shouting, "Arrest them, arrest them, I want them booked, the whole bunch of them. The black guy threatened me. He used bodily harm on me." I stood there worrying and wondering: Would they really put us in jail? Was the van ruined? What would happen to us now?

Of course, they found the radio right away. "Officer," J. P. said, "I'm really very sorry about this. I'm afraid my little girl has some emotional problems. Kleptomania. We've taken her to specialists; we've had her hypnotized; we've tried everything. We're desperate about it. Right now, we were headed for the Center for Disturbed Children in Trenton. You probably know about it. We hope they'll be able to do something."

To tell the truth, I was kind of ashamed of J. P. for telling such a story. I mean, if he was a great man, why did he have to stoop to stuff like that?

But the cops believed it—or at least they pretended they did and told us just to get out of their town. The manager went into a rage about that, but they told him that since he'd got his radio back, it wasn't worth the trouble to book us. So we went free.

But our van was ruined. We unloaded all the stuff from it into the other van—the camp stove, the orange plastic cooler, the cartons of amulets, honey, and pamphlets, the sleeping bags. We jammed it all into the Wiz's van and climbed in after it. With all that stuff in it, there was hardly any room for people, but J. P. and Trotsky squeezed into the front seat with the Wiz, and Gussie and Ooma and I squeezed ourselves in among the cartons and sleeping bags, and we drove away.

We were in a pretty big mess now. There wouldn't be room for all six of us to sleep in one van, that was sure. As we drove out of town, the grown-ups talked about it. Even an old, beat-up, second-hand van would cost a couple of thousand dollars at least— and probably more. We didn't have that kind of money, or anything like it, and no hope of getting it, either. Finally, they decided to head for a federal campground out in Pennsylvania that Trotsky knew about. It would be cheap and would have toilets and showers, and we could rig up some kind of shelter for some of us to sleep under out of a couple of tarpaulins we had. It seemed to me that things for us were getting worse and worse.

But the campground turned out to be a kind of nice place. It was all woods along the edge of a big lake. There were campsites carved out of the woods in such a way that every family of campers was screened off from the others. I wondered if I would have a chance to go fishing in the lake. Back on the old commune, we used to fish in our lake a lot. Trotsky was good at it, and she used to take me out in an old rowboat we had and show me how to put grasshoppers on a hook and how to cast the line out to where the fish might be. I hoped we could go out on the lake, if we could find a boat, and fish, if we could find something to fish with. I liked the idea of catching fish and eating them for supper.

We made a shelter out of a tarpaulin and set some of the cartons of honey and pamphlets around for chairs. We made a little fireplace out of stone, built a fire, and roasted potatoes in it, which was all we had for food. It was kind of nice sitting around that campfire roasting potatoes. I smelled the wood smoke from the fire and thought of those kids playing football. I kind of squashed the potato around in my mouth so it would seem like mashed potatoes.

After dinner I asked Trotsky if she would take me fishing. She said, "Let's go down to the lake and look over the lay of the land. Maybe there'll be a boat lying around loose somewhere."

I wasn't sure I wanted to get involved with stealing things again so soon. Trotsky believed in J. P.'s ideas and thought it was right to steal. She was stocky and wore her hair short and had glasses. Her big thing was junk sculpture. She knew how to weld and liked to make sculptures by welding junk together —hubcaps and bicycle wheels and pieces of chain and anything else she could find. Back on the old commune, you had to be careful about leaving your stuff around when she got into a welding mood, or the next thing you knew, your jackknife or your compass would be welded to her sculpture. Traveling around the way we were, she didn't get much chance to sculpt anything, but she collected things in case she did get the chance. Her and the Wiz's van was always rattling with hubcaps and bicycle wheels. The noise drove the Wiz crazy, and sometimes when it was Trotsky's turn to drive he would slip the rear doors open as the van was going along and shove some of the stuff out.

So Trotsky and I found a path through the woods and walked down to the lake. The sun was just setting behind the woods across the lake to our left, and the sky and the woods and the lake were all smeared with red.

"It's mighty pretty, isn't it, Fergy," Trotsky said. She put her hand up to shield her eyes and began looking along the shoreline for any signs of a boat.

I tried to think of something to say that would take her mind off stealing. "What do you think we're going to do about getting another van?"

She shrugged. "J. P. and the Wiz will figure out something," she said.

I knew what that meant. "Trotsky, I wish we didn't have to steal so much. We're liable to get in an awful lot of trouble."

"We just have to be more careful," she said. "Ooma hasn't got any sense. Whenever she sees something she wants, she just takes it. She's got to learn that the world isn't made that way. You can't have everything you want when you want it. She has to learn to postpone gratification, wait for the right moment before she leaps." She pointed along the shoreline. "That looks like a boat pulled up over there."

"It isn't only getting caught," I said. "I just don't like stealing."

Trotsky gave me a funny look. "What stealing?" she said. "We're just reclaiming what's rightfully ours. Don't you ever listen to anything your father says, Fergy?"

"I know all about that," I said. "I've heard it a thousand times. I just can't get myself to agree with it."

She gave a sigh and patted me on the back. "Confronting a crisis of faith, eh, fella? Well, don't worry about it. It's all part of growing up. Give it a little time, and you'll begin to see the justice of it."

FIVE

THE NEXT DAY it was kind of windy and rainy, and the rain blew in under the shelter we'd made out of tarps. We had to put the cartons back in the van and sit inside there all day. J. P. said he was going to go someplace and think the situation through, and the rest of us should tell each other stories to keep our spirits up, the way the Indians did. So the Wiz told a philosophical story about the death of Socrates, which made Ooma fidget. And Trotsky told a story about fighting in a revolution in South America, which was pretty exciting. And then Ooma told a story about a little princess who had two stereos and a pony and a color TV and her own van with a big bed in it just for herself. Ooma's story wasn't very good because nothing happened in it; it was just about the things that the little princess had.

All the time that Ooma was telling her story I was trying to think up one I could tell. For a long time I couldn't think of anything. Then I remembered a story I'd read in a book once about a boy who'd gone to some private school in England and had an emblem on his jacket and solved a murder and got famous for it.

Then it was Gussie's turn, and Ooma begged her to tell about when she was a little girl in that big house in Cambridge. So she told us about the shining silver and glistening glasses, and the maid serving the meals; about the gardener who came once a week to help her mother with the flowers; and about going to flower shows with her mother, where there would be so many beautiful flowers with such lovely smells that Gussie used to think that that was what heaven would be like; and about sitting in the big window seat in the upstairs hall on rainy Saturday mornings when her riding lesson was canceled and reading her favorite books all morning— *The Five Children and It* and *The Secret Garden* and *The Borrowers*. She was always having lessons, she said, so one of the nicest times for her was when she didn't have anything planned to do and could just be by herself and do what she wanted to do, like listen to the rain and read.

When she got finished I noticed that both Trotsky and the Wiz were staring at her. "It sounds to me like you miss all that, Gussie," Trotsky said.

"Of course I don't," Gussie snapped. "The kids like hearing about it, is all."

"Are you sure?" Trotsky said.

"Trotsky, the kids have a right to know about their own grandparents," Gussie said. "It's hard enough for them that they're not allowed to see them."

"Well, in any case," the Wiz said, trying to smooth the argument over, "I don't think it's necessarily a sound policy for the children to be given pretty pictures of so materialistic a way of life."

"Oh, Wiz," Gussie said. "Don't make such a big thing out of it. I don't think any of us would mind a little more materialism right now."

"Don't let it get you down, Gussie," Trotsky said. "J. P. will come up with something."

"Let's drop the subject," Gussie said. She looked kind of grim, which wasn't like her. She was right about one thing, though. I certainly would have liked to meet my grandparents. I was pretty curious about them, and so was Ooma. I mean, that richness and stuff got Ooma excited. For me, it wasn't so much the richness but the whole idea of a normal life—living in a house and eating regular food and taking showers all the time and stuff like that. I thought that it would be nice to visit our grandparents and be part of that for a while.

After that we played cards, only the six of diamonds and the jack of clubs were missing, so we couldn't play right. Finally, toward the end of the day it stopped raining and the sun came out a little, although it was still chilly. We got out of the van and stretched and ran around a little. Trotsky made a fire, and we took the cartons out of the van and sat on them around the fire; and just about the time that the fire was going well J. P. came back.

He sat down on a carton, sort of frowning and pulling at his mustache with one hand and poking a stick in the fire with the other, to make the sparks fly up. Nobody said anything; we knew that he was thinking something through. We talked in low tones so as not to bother his thinking. Finally, he cleared his throat, and we all stopped talking.

"I met some people," he said. He pointed with the stick into the woods. "They're camped over there. They're retired school teachers, maybe sixty-five. They're named Clappers, and they have a huge motor home. They spend all their time traveling. Spend a week here, a month there. He likes to fish, so they go where there are lakes a lot. New England in the summer; Florida, the Southwest in the winter. You should see the motor home they have—three-burner stove, refrigerator, table, bunks for four, wall-to-wall carpet, color TV. The works." He didn't say anything for a minute, and then he said, "I think we should get to know them." He looked at me. "Fergy, they've got a little rowboat they carry on the roof. Maybe you could get him to take you fishing."

I didn't like the idea of just asking a stranger to take

me out in his boat. "I don't have a fishing rod or anything."

"I'm sure he's got extra stuff," J. P. said. "There's no harm in asking. Just get friendly with him."

Well, it seemed kind of funny to me to make friends with somebody so you could ask them to take you fishing, especially when you would have to borrow hooks and line from them. But I liked the idea of going fishing, and I figured if we became friends with them, maybe he would ask me to go out with him.

But we had to get some money before we did anything, and the next day we left Ooma and Gussie in the campsite to watch the stuff we were keeping under the canvas shelter and the rest of us went into a nearby town and worked a couple of shopping malls. We picked up nearly fifty bucks. J. P. decided we needed something to lift our spirits, so he spent most of the money on a couple of big steaks, some French fries, and a bottle of wine for the grown-ups. We got back to the campsite and made a fire, and then J. P. told me and Ooma to go over to visit the people he'd met and see if they would lend us mustard for the steaks.

I didn't like borrowing any more than I did stealing. "Maybe they won't have any," I said.

Ooma grabbed my sleeve. "Come on, Fergy," she said. "I want to see their big motor home."

"You better not swipe anything."

"I won't. I just want to see it."

There was a path through the woods leading from our campsite to theirs. We went along it. It was about five o'clock, and the sun streamed down through the trees. Squirrels and chipmunks darted along through the leaves on the ground and scooted up trees when they saw us coming. Birds were twittering, too. It was pretty nice being there, and I wondered if we'd be able to stay for a while. Especially if I got a chance to go fishing.

It only took us a couple of minutes to get to the motor home. It was parked in a clearing in the woods just the way our van was. It was something, all right. It looked as big as a freight car. There was a little folding table under the awning, a couple of chairs around the table, and sitting on one of the chairs was Mr. Clappers. He was wearing old khakis, glasses, and he had a twist of white hair that kind of stuck up from his head like a twirl of whipped cream. A fishing rod was lying on the ground next to him. The reel was in pieces on the table in front of him. He was picking up the pieces one at a time and wiping them with a rag and some oil.

When we came out of the woods he looked up and smiled. "Hello," he said.

"Hi," I said. "Mr. Clappers?"

"That's me," he said. "What's your name?"

"Fergy Wheeler," I said. "My father—"

He didn't pay any attention to what I was saying, but looked at Ooma. "And who are you?"

Ooma stared at him, but she didn't say anything.

"She doesn't have very good manners," I said. "She's sort of wild." I nudged her. "Tell him your name."

"Ooma," she said.

"That's an unusual name."

I thought it was nice of him not to say that it was weird. "It's an Indian name," I said.

"What sort of Indians?"

"I don't know," I said. "Some Indian language that the Wiz knows about. It's supposed to mean 'filled with sweetness and light.' "

Mr. Clappers set down the piece of reel he was oiling and examined Ooma. "Are you really filled with sweetness and light?"

"No," she said. "That's a load of crap. I'm always getting into trouble."

He went on looking at her, like she was an interesting

problem that he wanted to puzzle out. "Yes, I can imagine that," he said. "What kind of trouble do you get into, mostly?"

"I rob stuff," she said.

I turned red. I wished she hadn't said that. Mr. Clappers seemed like he might like us and maybe take me fishing. "Ooma—"

"Is that true, Fergy?"

"I guess so," I said. "She doesn't mean anything by it. She just can't help herself."

"Oh?" He leaned back and put his hands behind his head. I figured that being as he was retired he had plenty of time to puzzle things like Ooma out. "What kind of things do you steal, Ooma?"

Ooma gave me a confused look. She wasn't used to anybody being so calm about her stealing. She looked back at Mr. Clappers. "I don't know," she said.

"It isn't usually much," I lied. "Clark Bars. Stuff like that."

"I took this big radio a couple of days ago," she said. "It was *this* big."

I wished she could keep her mouth shut. "She only takes stuff like that sometimes."

Mr. Clappers said, "What do you steal for, Ooma? Do you need the money?"

Her face got confused again. She looked down at her shoes. "I don't know," she said. "It makes me feel better."

"It's kind of a habit," I said.

Mr. Clappers laughed. "Well, it's not a very good habit to get into. You're likely to land in jail."

Just then, a woman came out of the rear door of the motor home and down the little steps. She was sort of plump and had a round face and glasses and white hair all fluffed up around her head. "Who are you talking

43

to, Edgar?'' Then she saw us. "Oh," she said. "What a pretty little girl."

"Her name's Ooma," Mr. Clappers said. "She steals."

"I'm sure that's not true, not a pretty little thing like her. How would you kids like a can of soda? I'm sure you would, wouldn't you?" She went back into the motor home and came out with two cans of Sprite. She was also carrying a wet washcloth. "Here you are," she said, handing us the Sprites. "Now, Ooma, I'm just going to wash off a little of that dirt so I can see how pretty you really are."

That was going to be a mistake. "Maybe you better not," I said. "Sometimes she bites people when they try to wash her."

"I'm sure she won't." Mrs. Clappers knelt down in front of Ooma and ran the washcloth over her face. Ooma spluttered and tried to curse through the washcloth, but, amazingly enough, she didn't bite or hit. She just stood there letting Mrs. Clappers do it. "There," Mrs. Clappers said. She stepped back a little and cocked her head, like she was looking at a painting to see if she'd got it right. "That's much better."

Ooma was looking kind of shocked. She was as surprised as I was that she'd let Mrs. Clappers wash her face without taking a bite out of her hand. Ooma reached up and rubbed her cheek to see if it felt any different. The whole thing was making me feel kind of funny. I mean, I felt good, but funny—some kind of feeling I didn't understand. I stood there frowning and trying to get hold of it, but it kept coming and going the way feelings do, hard to catch as a butterfly. Then I realized that the steaks must be done and we better get back. "Mrs. Clappers, J. P. asked if we could borrow some mustard."

"J. P.?" Mr. Clappers said. "Who's J. P.?"

"That's our dad."

44

"Oh," Mr. Clappers said. "That the plump gent with the mustache who stopped by yesterday?"

"Yes. He wanted to know if we could borrow—"

"Seemed like an interesting gent," Mr. Clappers said. "We had a long philosophical discourse about the evils of the system."

"J. P.'s supposed to be a great philosopher. He's writing a book called *The Journals of J. P. Wheeler*. It's going to be famous someday." Suddenly I wished I hadn't said that. I always believed that J. P. was a great philosopher, but saying the words right out, so I heard them in my ears, it sounded sort of foolish. I went hot and prickly. "Anyway, that's what they say."

Mr. Clappers nodded. "I'm sure he will be."

"Now, Edgar," Mrs. Clappers said. "These children came over to borrow some mustard, not to entertain you. They have to get back. I'll just get a jar of mustard for them." She went back into the motor home.

I decided to get the conversation around to fishing. "Is that a fishing reel?" I said, pointing to the parts on the table.

"It will be if I ever get it back together again," he said. "You like to fish?"

"I used to, when we lived on the old com—when I was little." I didn't understand why I felt ashamed to tell him about the old commune. "Just with a hand line, mostly. Trot—somebody used to take me out in an old boat we had."

"Well, Fergy, you'd better come fishing with me sometime."

"Sure," I said. "Only I don't have any fishing stuff."

"I'm sure I can dig up some tackle," he said.

Then Mrs. Clappers came out with the mustard, and we went on back through the woods to our campsite. All the way along, I kept trying to puzzle out what that funny feeling was that I'd got from talking to Mr. and Mrs. Clappers. Then we got back to the campsite.

"What took you so long?" Gussie said.

"Mr. Clappers is kind of talky," I said. "He asks a lot of questions."

J. P. nodded. "You got to be friendly with them?"

"She washed my face," Ooma said.

Gussie looked surprised. "Washed your face?"

"I kind of liked it," Ooma said.

Gussie frowned at J. P. "I don't think she had a right to do that. Doesn't she think I keep the child clean enough?"

"Oh, don't worry about it, Gussie," J. P. said. "She was only trying to be friendly."

"He said he would take me fishing," I said. "He said he'd dig up some tackle for me."

J. P. grunted. "So you're making friends with them. I figured as much. They taught school for years and miss having kids around. Ooma, just see that you don't cause any trouble with them. Hear me?"

SIX

THE NEXT MORNING after breakfast, J. P. told
Ooma and me to bring the jar of mustard back to Mr.
and Mrs. Clappers. We went off through the woods
with it. It was another nice day, with the sun falling
through the trees and the birds flashing through the sun
and the little animals racing over the dead leaves and
shooting up into trees when we came by. We got to the
motor home. Nobody was sitting at the table under the
awning, so I went up the little steps and looked through
the window in the door. Mr. and Mrs. Clappers were
eating breakfast and watching the news on TV. I was
amazed at how much stuff they had in there—a good-
sized table and a sofa that I figured turned into a bed,
and an easy chair, and an icebox and everything else. I
knocked. Mr. Clappers looked up and saw us. He waved
us to come in. I opened the door. The air was filled
with the smell of eggs and coffee and English muffins
with butter on them. All we had had for breakfast was
doughnuts and Coke. "We brought you back the mustard," I said.

"Oh, you should have kept it," Mrs. Clappers said.

"Come in, come in," Mr. Clappers shouted from the
table. "Have you had your breakfast? How about a
muffin?"

"Well—" I said.

"Boy, would I love some damn eggs," Ooma said.
"We never get eggs."

47

"Ooma—"

"Oh, that's all right, Fergy," Mrs. Clappers said. "Come on in."

So we went in. Mrs. Clappers made us some eggs and gave us each an English muffin with strawberry jam while we were waiting for the eggs to cook. While we ate, Mr. Clappers gave me a long talk about fishing. He said that the lake was full of bass; he'd almost caught one two feet long, but it broke the line and got away. "You have to come out with me. Maybe we'll go this evening. The best time is dusk." Well, I wanted to go, all right, so I said I'd ask J. P. Then we finished up our eggs, and I said thanks and made Ooma say thanks, and we started back. As we were going down the steps I heard Mrs. Clappers say, "They're really nice kids. It's a shame they're not growing up in a better environment." I got that funny feeling again—nice, but strange. I couldn't understand it.

This time we left Ooma and Trotsky to look after the campsite, and the rest of us went out and worked a couple of shopping malls. We didn't do too bad, but the problem was, J. P. said, we were too far out in the country, and pretty soon we'd work the area out. We couldn't stay at that campground forever.

That disappointed me. I liked being there in the woods with the little animals dashing around and maybe getting a chance to go fishing in that lake. And, to tell the truth, it was nice getting to know normal people like Mr. and Mrs. Clappers. Of course, I didn't really know what normal people were like; I'd never known any. But I'd read about them in books and seen pictures of them in magazine advertisements, and I had a pretty good idea of how they lived. The thing about normal people was that they were all part of the same thing. They all had turkey on Thanksgiving and firecrackers on the Fourth of July and noisemakers on New Year's

Eve. We didn't believe in the Fourth of July because it was a celebration of war, and on Thanksgiving we usually had hot dogs or something, because how could you cook a turkey on a camp stove in a van? Normal people all belonged to something. We didn't belong to anything except ourselves.

Anyway, J. P. said I could go fishing with Mr. Clappers, and I did. He caught a bass and I caught a sunny. My sunny was too small to keep, but I didn't mind. I didn't mind that at all. I liked sitting there in that little fiberglass rowboat, watching the sun go down behind the trees at the edge of the lake, feeling the night breeze come up, and talking to Mr. Clappers. It was so easy and peaceful that I didn't care if I caught anything at all.

Mr. Clappers certainly had a curious streak. He asked me a lot of questions about how we made our money, if Ooma and I went to school, and where Gussie and J. P. came from and all that. It was embarrassing to me, because I knew that it would sound pretty weird to him.

He took it all in like it was normal to live in a beat-up van and not go to school and have a sister who stole. But it surprised me when he said, "It must be sort of fun to live that way and not go to school, Fergy."

I didn't know what to answer. I felt like telling the truth and saying that it wasn't fun, that I was scared about being so dumb and tired of never being normal. But I didn't want it to sound like I hated my own parents or was against J. P.'s ideas. So I said, "I guess it's okay."

He flipped the line out in the direction of the setting sun, and I saw the spinner fall into the top of the sun and fall out again at the bottom and plop into the water. "Your dad must be a pretty smart guy," he said.

I didn't want to talk about J. P.'s journals to Mr. Clappers anymore. "I guess so," I said.

He began to turn the reel slowly, working the spinner backward toward the boat. "I guess you'd like to be like him when you grow up," he said.

I looked over the side of the boat like I was seeing a fish. "I guess so," I said. I wished he would stop asking so many questions, and he did. He began talking about where the fish might be biting better, and I began to feel good again. When it got dark we went in. I had a Coke at his motor home, and then I went back to our campsite.

The next day it was the Wiz's turn to stay home and watch over the campsite. As for Ooma, J. P. said she could spend the day with Mr. and Mrs. Clappers. "They like kids. They won't mind having her." Then he told Ooma, "You better be good, or I'm going to wallop you." It was surprising to me that J. P. was allowing us to be down at the Clapperses' so much. Usually, he didn't like us to spend too much time with regular people, in case we picked up their ideas.

After that, Ooma got to going down there every day and staying all day. The first thing she wanted when she got there was to have Mrs. Clappers wash her face and hands, tuck her shirt into her jeans, and tidy her up generally. It even got to where Mrs. Clappers gave Ooma a shampoo and put her hair up in pigtails. Ooma was mighty proud of them, and she stood in front of the mirror they had in the bathroom of the motor home, turning her head from side to side to make her pigtails swing.

Gussie frowned when she saw the pigtails. "I didn't know you wanted pigtails, Ooma," she said. "Why didn't you tell me? You didn't have to get Mrs. Clappers to do it."

"It's all right, Gussie," J. P. said. "It's a good thing for them to be friendly with the kids. There's no harm in it."

Gussie went on frowning. "What does she think, I can't take care of my own children? It doesn't look right." I could tell that she was worried about it, but she didn't say anything more.

I couldn't get to the Clapperses' too often because I had to go around to shopping malls, but usually I went down there in the evenings. If the weather was right, Mr. Clappers took me fishing, and if it was bad, we sat around the motor home watching TV and eating cookies. Mrs. Clappers said it was a pleasure having children around, it had been years since she'd had anyone to bake cookies for, and she missed it. "Not since Teddy grew up," she said.

"Who's Teddy?" Ooma said, with her mouth full of cookies.

Mr. and Mrs. Clappers looked at each other. Then Mrs. Clappers said, "Teddy was our son. He was killed in Vietnam." She opened a bureau drawer and took out a picture of a man in an army uniform, smiling, and showed it to us.

"Is he dead?" Ooma said.

"Yes, I'm afraid so, Ooma," Mrs. Clappers said. I knew I ought to say I was sorry, or something, but I felt too shy. So I just looked at the picture, and in a minute Mr. Clappers changed the subject back to fishing, and Mrs. Clappers put the picture away.

We went on this way for a few days, and around the end of the fifth or sixth day I began to get some pretty funny ideas. What would it be like to live with Mr. and Mrs. Clappers? They had four bunks in the motor home, and it seemed like they had plenty of money. I mean, a motor home like that cost thousands and thousands of dollars, so they couldn't be poor.

Besides, they were teachers. They'd both taught in the same school for years. Mr. Clappers had taught social studies and Mrs. Clappers had taught science. I figured they knew enough to teach anything—English, history, math, anything.

I began thinking about that a lot. I would lie in my sleeping bag at night listening to the peepers—and wondering. If we lived with the Clapperses, would they get tired of us after a while and stop being nice? Would Ooma start stealing from them? Or would it always be nice?

I wondered what Ooma would think about it. I wanted to ask her, but I was afraid of putting ideas in her head, because she might blurt something out to J. P. and Gussie. But then, one night as we were walking through the woods back to our campsite, she brought it up herself.

"Mrs. Clappers said we could stay for dinner," she said.

"Did she?"

"She was making pork chops and said she had plenty. Pork chops and applesauce and mashed potatoes. I wish we could have stayed."

"I don't think we should bother them all the time," I said.

"Mrs. Clappers said they like it when we come to visit them."

Neither of us said anything, but walked on through the woods, with the sun going down behind us and the shadows coming up into the woods. Then she said, "Fergy, do you think if we asked them they'd let us live with them?"

"I don't think we ought to," I said. "J. P. and Gussie would have their feelings hurt."

"I don't give a damn if they do," she said. "Do you think we could, Fergy?"

I sure wanted to. "I don't know, Ooma. I'll think about it. Just don't bring it up to anybody."

A couple of mornings after that, I took Ooma through

the woods to the Clapperses' campsite as usual, around eight o'clock. Mr. and Mrs. Clappers were having breakfast. Ooma just slid into her seat next to Mrs. Clappers, who began to serve out some scrambled eggs and bacon. "How about you, Fergy?" she said.

"I have to get back," I said.

"Take a prune Danish, anyway," she said. "I made them this morning." She passed me the plate, and I took one. It was still hot from the oven and smelled wonderful.

"Fergy," Mr. Clappers said, "how would you and Ooma like to go on a picnic tonight? There's an island a couple of miles down the lake covered with pines. We were thinking of going down there in the boat around five o'clock and having supper while it's still light."

The funny thing was, going on a picnic was no big thing for me. I'd spent most of my life on picnics—camping someplace and eating sandwiches or cooking hot dogs over the camp stove. For me, the most fun would be to go into a regular house and eat supper on a table. So the picnic part wouldn't be very interesting to me. But going someplace with Mr. and Mrs. Clappers would be nice—it would be like living with them for a little while. "I have to ask J. P.," I said.

"Well, you ask him," Mrs. Clappers said. "You tell him we invited you two especially."

So when I got back to our campsite I did, and he said, "Fine, by all means, stay as long as you like; I'm sure you'll be in good hands with them. No rush about getting back." And that night around five o'clock, I went through the woods to their campsite. They were ready and waiting for me. They were pretty cheerful—both of them talking at the same time, and Ooma just as excited as she could be, opening up the picnic basket and showing me all the things that were in it. "Look, Fergy, deviled eggs and ham sandwiches and macaroni

53

salad and goat cheese—*fffyyck*—and brownies and pickles and cake. I helped on the deviled eggs. You mash up the yellow part with mayonnaise and mustard and stuff and jam it back inside.'' Oh, she was excited, all right, even though she'd spent all of her life on picnics, just like me.

We walked through the woods to the lake. Mr. Clappers carried the little outboard motor for the boat, I carried the picnic basket, and Mrs. Clappers carried a blanket. The boat was just big enough to hold us. Mrs. Clappers had the whole front to herself because of being plump, and Mr. Clappers sat in the rear running the motor. We kept tipping from Ooma's squirming around, and Mr. Clappers kept shouting out ''Trim the ship'' and singing some song called ''Oh, the Life of a Sailor,'' until Mrs. Clappers told him to stop it, he sang like a horse, he never could sing, and there wasn't any use in trying to learn now. The sun was still up in the sky. A little breeze ruffled the water, and, up above, gulls were circling and wheeling and squabbling among themselves. All of a sudden I just filled with happiness. I don't know what it was, but it just came over me and I sat there feeling it all, happy as I'd ever been. I couldn't remember a time when I'd been so happy.

We got to the island and pulled the boat up onto the beach. Then we climbed up into the pine forest a little bit. Oh, it smelled just beautiful there. The ground was covered with needles, soft as a cushion, and through the trees we could see the sun sparkling on the lake, like flakes of gold. ''It's pretty here, isn't it, Fergy?'' Mr. Clappers said.

''It sure is,'' I said. I still felt happy. ''It's the prettiest place I've ever seen.''

''Let's spread out the blanket so we can get at the grub,'' he said.

So we did, and Ooma and Mrs. Clappers unpacked

the food and the paper plates and plastic forks and stuff. "This is how to live, isn't it?" Mr. Clappers said.

It was, all right. "Everything smells so good," I said.

We sat and ate, and Mr. Clappers told us about all the places they'd been—the Grand Canyon, the Everglades in Florida where they had real alligators, Carlsbad Caverns; and we told them about places we'd been. In between times, I told Ooma to stop talking with her mouth full and not to eat with her fingers.

"Fergy," Mr. Clappers said, "you've got a long way to go with Ooma's table manners."

"She's just a child," Mrs. Clappers said. "Give her time."

Finally, we were full and got sort of quiet and just sat there looking out through the trees at the water. The sun was going down now. "It's going to get chilly soon," Mrs. Clappers said.

We were quiet again, and then suddenly Ooma blurted out, "I wish we could live with you."

"Ooma," I said.

Mr. and Mrs. Clappers didn't say anything, but looked at each other. Finally, Mrs. Clappers said, "We talked about that a little, Ooma."

"It's not something you do without giving it a lot of thought," Mr. Clappers said.

I couldn't believe it. Did they really want us to come and live with them? Could we really do it? "I don't know if J. P. and Gussie would let us," I said.

"We could run away," Ooma said.

"It's not that easy," Mr. Clappers said. "A thing like that would be up to the parents."

I wondered: Would J. P. and Gussie ever agree to it? I wasn't sure. It didn't seem likely, but maybe they would. "I don't know if they would like the idea."

Mr. Clappers looked at me. "What do you think of it, Fergy?"

I didn't know what to say. I knew it was wrong to say that I didn't want to live with my own family anymore. Ooma was too young to understand that, but I knew that it was wrong. Kids were supposed to want to stay with their families, for if they didn't want to, it meant that there was something wrong with their parents. Still, I didn't want to mess up the chance. "Well, if J. P. and Gussie would agree, I think I would."

Nobody said anything for a minute, and then Mr. Clappers nodded and said, "Let's just think about it for a while."

It was getting dark, and a breeze was coming up. I shivered. "We'd better get going while there's still some light," Mr. Clappers said. We packed all the plates and jars and forks into the picnic basket, folded up the blanket, went down to the boat, and headed back for the campgrounds. We were all sort of quiet, even Ooma. I sat next to her in the middle of the boat, wondering if it really would happen. What would J. P. and Gussie say if we asked them? Would they ever let us go?

We got back to our beach, hauled the boat up, and locked it to a tree with a chain. Then we walked up through the woods toward the Clapperses' motor home, carrying the stuff. It was pretty dark now, and we couldn't see the motor home through the woods. "That's funny," Mrs. Clappers said. "I thought I left a light on so we could find our way back."

"I thought you did, too," Mr. Clappers said. "Maybe the bulb burned out." We kept on coming and then we reached the Clapperses' campsite. There was no moon yet, but the stars were bright. We stood at the edge of the clearing in the faint shadows of the trees, staring. The motor home was gone.

SEVEN

WE STOOD THERE staring with our mouths open. It was like a house had suddenly disappeared. In the faint light, we could see the oblong patch of dead grass where the motor home had been. That was all. "I don't believe it," Mr. Clappers said. "Who on earth could have taken it? How do they think they're going to get away with it?"

"Are you sure you locked it?" Mrs. Clappers said.

Mr. Clappers reached in his pocket, took out his keys, and stared at them in the starlight. "Pretty sure," he said.

But I'd seen J. P. pick locks with pieces of wire and files. I felt terrible—sick and weak and ashamed. All that business about us getting to be friends of Mr. and Mrs. Clappers was just to get them away from the motor home for a while. It wouldn't have taken long—maybe fifteen minutes to pick the lock and get into the motor home, and another fifteen minutes to cross the wires in the ignition system so they could start the engine. I'd seen J. P. do that, too.

Mr. Clappers set down the outboard motor, went over to the oblong patch of dead grass, and squatted down, looking for clues. There wouldn't be any, I knew. J. P. was smart. I wondered what they'd done with it—driven off a good ways from there and hidden it down a woods road or something. As soon as we went back to our campsite, they'd grab Ooma and me and we'd take off.

When Mr. and Mrs. Clappers realized that we'd taken off in the night without even saying good-bye, they'd know who'd taken their motor home, and they'd think we'd been in on the whole thing. After that, they'd hate us. Oh, I felt awful. But there was nothing I could say.

Mr. Clappers stood up and walked back to where the rest of us were standing in the starlit shadows of the woods. "Fergy, your folks must have heard them drive away. Maybe they know something. Let's go up and ask them. We have to get somebody to give us a ride into town to the police station, anyway."

I didn't want to see J. P. I didn't want to see him or Gussie or any of them. "I don't know if they would have heard anything."

"Maybe not," Mr. Clappers said. "But let's ask. Anyway, somebody can give us a lift into town."

He started off through the woods toward our campsite, and there wasn't anything to do but follow him. Mrs. Clappers came along behind, holding Ooma by the hand. I could see the flickering of a campfire up ahead and hear the sounds of voices. In a minute, we came out into the clearing where the van was. They'd got a fire going, and J. P. was bent over it, grilling a couple of steaks. I figured they'd taken the steaks out of the Clapperses' freezer.

When J. P. saw us come out of the woods he straightened up. "Hello, there," he said. "We were wondering where you'd gone to. We heard the motor home start up a little while ago."

Mr. Clappers walked over to him. Now I could see his face in the light from the fire. He looked terrible, like somebody had died. I remembered that picture of their son. They would never see him anymore. "That wasn't us," he said. "We were out on the lake the whole time. Somebody stole it."

"Stole it?" J. P. said. He straightened up and looked Mr. Clappers in the face. He really seemed surprised.

58

"Your trailer was stolen?" Trotsky said. She sounded surprised, too, and she came up to Mr. Clappers. I stood at the edge of the clearing. I wanted to be as far away from them as I could. Mrs. Clappers stood at the edge of the clearing, too, holding Ooma's hand. Then I noticed that the Wiz wasn't there. I figured he was driving as fast as he could out of the state in the motor home to someplace where we would meet him in a day or so.

"How long ago did you hear it?" Mr. Clappers asked J. P.

"Well, come to think of it, it could have been as much as an hour ago. I didn't notice the time, actually."

"It was at least an hour ago," Trotsky said. "I remember wondering about it. I remember wondering if you were taking the kids into town for ice cream or something." It was amazing to me what a good act they were putting on. They almost convinced me that they hadn't stolen it, after all. Maybe I was wrong; maybe I was just jumping to conclusions. But I didn't think so.

Now I realized that Gussie wasn't joining in. She was sitting in the back of the van with her legs crossed, her chin in her hand. I wondered if she and J. P. had had a fight about something.

"It could be just kids joyriding," J. P. said. "Maybe it'll turn up in the morning by the side of the road somewhere."

Mr. Clappers shook his head. "I doubt it," he said. "There's a pretty good lock on the door. It would have taken an expert to pick it."

J. P. shrugged. "They could have busted a window and got in that way."

"I thought of that," Mr. Clappers said. "I checked the ground. I didn't find any broken glass."

J. P. remembered the steaks and flipped them over on the grill. "Well, at least you've got insurance," he said.

59

"Oh, yes, we're covered," Mr. Clappers said. "We can get the money back. But that place was our home. We liked it. It's got a lot of irreplaceable stuff in it—our clothes, my favorite fishing rod, photographs."

I remembered the picture of his son again.

"Maybe you'll get some of that stuff back. Sometimes thieves dump stuff like that."

I wondered if there was any way I could send them that picture. At least that. It would be terrible for them not even to have a picture of their son anymore. But where would I send it to? I went on standing by the edge of the clearing, feeling awful. I wanted to turn around and run away, run down through the woods and keep on running as fast and as far away as I could go until I was gone from them. I wanted to go someplace where they could never find me. For suddenly I didn't believe any of it anymore. I didn't believe that J. P. was a great man and that his journals were going to be famous someday. I didn't believe that we had a right to steal anything we wanted. I didn't believe that the system was responsible for all our troubles. Mr. and Mrs. Clappers weren't any system, they were just plain people, and they didn't deserve to have their motor home stolen from them just because we needed it.

But I couldn't run, because the minute I did, Mr. and Mrs. Clappers would realize that something funny was going on. They would begin to guess that we had stolen their motor home, and then there was no telling what J. P. would do. He might decide to do something bad to them so we could make our escape. So I went on standing at the edge of the clearing in the starlight.

The steaks were done, and J. P. took them off the fire. "Ooma, Fergy, come get something to eat."

There wasn't any way I was going to touch a bite of that steak. "I'm not hungry," I said. "I had plenty to eat before."

"Well, I am," he said. He got out one of our tin plates, sat down on a carton, and began to eat. I figured he'd missed his supper because he'd been busy with the Wiz stealing the motor home. "There's another steak," he said. "Anybody want it? Trotsky? Gussie? How about it, Gussie?"

She went on sitting in the van. She didn't say anything, just shook her head. So Trotsky got another plate and sat down and ate the steak. Mr. Clappers went on talking to J. P. about who might have taken the motor home, and what they ought to do next. And finally, it was arranged that Trotsky would drive them into town, so they could report the theft to the police and find a motel to stay in. Mrs. Clappers gave Ooma a hug, and they both waved to me, but they had too much on their minds to worry about us particularly. They didn't realize that they would never see us again. So off they went with Trotsky, and I went on standing in the starlight at the edge of the clearing.

Now J. P. realized that something was wrong with me. He finished his steak and came on over to me. "What's the matter with you, Fergy?"

"You stole the motor home."

Suddenly Gussie shouted out from the back of the van, "I told you, J. P."

J. P. snapped his head around. "You stay out of it, Gussie," he shouted. He looked back at me. "Fergy—"

"I told you, J. P.," Gussie shouted again. "I told you you were going too far."

"You let me handle this," he shouted over his shoulder. He looked back at me. Then he said, "We needed it. They have plenty of money. They have big pensions and social security. What right have the two of them to ride around in a big motor home like that while the six of us are crammed into one crummy van?"

He always had a way of putting things that confused

61

me. But I was determined not to let him confuse me this time. "They worked for it," I said. Ooma realized that we were talking about Mr. and Mrs. Clappers, and she came over to us.

"That's the point, Fergy. They were willing to work for the system. We won't. We refuse to contribute to a system that's based on materialism and war. That's why we don't have any money. You can't expect the system to reward us for challenging it, can you?"

Ooma put her thumb in her mouth. "They wanted us to come and live with them."

I wished she hadn't said that. "I don't think they were serious," I said. But I knew they had been.

"Yes, they were," Ooma said. "They meant it."

J. P. looked from one of us to the other in the starlight. "Live with them? Why, of all the damn nerve. First they swagger around flaunting their wealth, and then they try to steal our children." He gave me a hard look. "What made you think we'd ever allow that, Fergy?"

I could see now that the whole idea had been crazy. There was never a chance that J. P. and Gussie would let us go. "I don't know," I said. "I guess I didn't. It was just an idea."

He stared at me. "Would you have wanted to do that—leave us to live with strangers?"

Why couldn't Ooma have kept her mouth shut? How was I going to answer a question like that? Could I tell him that I didn't believe in him anymore? Could I tell him that I hated him for stealing the motor home? Could I tell him that I wanted to get as far away from him as I could? "They didn't mean it. It was just an idea."

"Yes, they did too mean it," Ooma said. She just didn't have any sense.

J. P. looked at her. "Would you have wanted that, Ooma—to leave us and live with the Clapperses?"

Suddenly she looked confused. She kept her thumb in her mouth, and her eyes looked around in the dark.

"Would you, Ooma?"

She shook her head, but she didn't take her thumb out of her mouth or say anything. Suddenly J. P. put his arms around our shoulders. "Look, you two guys stop worrying about it. Let me do the worrying. Mr. and Mrs. Clappers have got insurance; they'll get another motor home. We were within our rights to reclaim it. Just think how much fun we're going to have with it."

I wasn't going to have much fun in it. I was going to feel lousy about being in it, for I would keep remembering Mrs. Clappers ladling out eggs and English muffins, and going fishing with Mr. Clappers. So I went and sat by the fire and stared into the flames, feeling confused and upset and wanting to cry more than anything, but not wanting to let J. P. know I was crying.

Trotsky came back with the van an hour later. We put out the fire, loaded our stuff into the van, and left the campsite. "Where are we going to?" Ooma said.

"You'll see," J. P. said. I knew he didn't want to say, because he was suspicious of me.

"Is the motor home ours now?" Ooma said.

"Yes," J. P. said.

"Do you hear that, Fergy?" she said.

I didn't say anything.

"You kids get some sleep," J. P. said. "It's late." He didn't want us getting into a conversation about it—that was clear. I was sick of him now, sick of stealing and sick of not being able to go to school and sick of all these lies about the system and J. P.'s great journals. All at once I knew I had to run away.

EIGHT

IT TOOK US three days to catch up to the Wiz. He'd raced out of Pennsylvania in a couple of hours that night and then wandered around through Delaware, Maryland, Virginia, and North Carolina until he was sure that nobody was following him. Then he'd driven into Spartanburg, South Carolina, and we met him there. J. P. and the Wiz bought some paint and changed the color of the motor home. They scraped off the Clapperses' stickers saying GRAND CANYON, THE EVERGLADES, CARLSBAD CAVERNS, and so forth. Changing the registration was going to be more of a problem, though. J. P. and the Wiz talked about it. To get a new registration they would have to turn in the old one, which had the engine number on it. The chances were that it would be on some computer list of stolen vehicles and they'd be caught right there in the motor vehicle office. But they didn't have to face that problem yet, for the old registration had a couple of months to run.

So J. P., Gussie, Ooma, and I moved into the motor home, and the Wiz and Trotsky had the other van all to themselves. We ate all our meals together in the motor home. Ooma was kind of thrilled about the whole thing. She seemed to have forgotten about Mrs. Clappers's washing her face and putting her hair in pigtails and giving her breakfast every day. She got a kick out of sitting at the table playing cards or drinking a Coke while we were driving along. J. P. got a kick out of it, too. He liked driving it because the seat was high up and he could look down on the other cars that went by. He liked sitting there in the evening with a beer, watching the news on TV and pointing out to all of us what the system was doing to everybody. He was proud of having that fancy motor home, and sometimes as he drove along he'd get to singing—"Blowin' in the Wind," "Hey Jude," "Mrs. Robinson," stuff like that.

But I couldn't stand it, and J. P. knew it. A couple of times he gave me a talking-to. The talking-tos didn't work. I still felt rotten about stealing something from people who'd been so nice to us, and sick that they were bound to think that Ooma and I were in on it and had double-crossed them. Finally, after I would hardly talk to anybody for two or three days, J. P. blew up at me. "What makes you think you know all the answers, Fergy? What makes you think you're so smart? Now, you cut out this sulking and grow up a little bit, or I'm going to do something about it."

Suddenly Gussie said, "Leave him alone, J. P."

"I don't want to get it from you, either, Gussie," J. P. said.

"You went too far this time, J. P.," she said. "Keep it in mind that we're all accomplices in this."

"That's right," he snapped. "We're a family. We're all in it together. That's the way it ought to be in a family."

"If we're going to all be in it together, how about letting the rest of us in on the decisions every once in a while?"

"I'm not going to argue with you about it," J. P. said. Gussie didn't say anything more about it, and neither did he, and for a while nobody said anything, until Ooma asked Gussie for something to eat. But I didn't care, for I wasn't going to be living with them much longer.

The trouble was, I didn't have anyplace to run away *to*. There wasn't any use in just running away and living in the streets: It had to be someplace where I could go to a regular school and live a regular life and get into the Boy Scouts and the school band and be on some team. But where?

Suddenly it came to me: Gussie's parents. They had plenty of money and a big house with lots of rooms in it—at least they had had all that once, fifteen years before when Gussie had run away. Maybe they would be glad to have their grandson come and live with them. It would be some surprise for them. I didn't think they even knew about me, or Ooma. Had Gussie ever written them a letter about us? I decided it would be a good idea to find out as much about them as I could. Maybe they didn't live in that big house anymore. Maybe they didn't even live in Cambridge. They could even be dead. But I wanted to find out about them as quick as I could. We were heading generally westward. J. P. had decided that it would be best to get out into sparsely settled country like Oklahoma or Wyoming, so we were working our way through Tennessee toward Arkansas, and from there planning to angle off to the Northwest. The longer I waited to run away, the farther from Cambridge I would be.

So, over the next couple of days I pretended to have got over my sulks and be feeling better again, and I began asking questions, like I was just trying to while away the time. "Gussie, when you were a kid, did you have your own room?"

"Oh, you don't want to hear all that stuff again, do you?"

"Yes, we do," Ooma said.

"I should think you'd be bored of it by now."

"No, we're not bored. Tell us," Ooma said.

"Yes, I had my own room. We had a big house with lots of rooms."

"How big was it?" Ooma said. She didn't realize how helpful she was being to me by asking questions.

"Oh, it was big," Gussie said. "A big, white clapboard house with a porch running along the front. There was a little yard in front with an iron rail fence going along the sidewalk. There was a gate in the fence and a flagstone walk coming up through the little yard. Sometimes, on hot summer nights, we would sit on the porch and watch the people walking along the sidewalk. We would eat strawberry ice cream out of glasses full of ginger ale. We had long silver spoons with handles like straws. You could eat the ice cream with the spoon or suck it up through the silver straw. My father liked strawberry ice cream, so we always had it."

"How could you see the people going along in the dark?" Ooma said.

"There was a streetlight right in front of the house. I remember that streetlight, because my room was on the front of the house and the streetlight shone in at night when I was going to sleep. I liked that, because even when my mother pulled down the shade, some light glowed through it so the room wasn't so dark and scary."

"Were you scared of the dark when you were little?" Ooma said.

"Oh, yes," Gussie said. She had a kind of faraway, dreamy look in her eyes. "I always thought something was out there in the dark. A big, old wooden house like that creaks at night as the boards cool down. I'd hear that creaking and I'd think it was an evil being coming across the floorboards to get me. Or when the wind blew the branches around in the streetlight, the shadows would jump off the wall toward me, and if I was half-asleep I'd jerk awake and scream, and my mother would have to come into my room and hug me until I calmed down."

I thought she might stop, so I asked a question my-self. "Why wouldn't they let you have your light on?" I said.

"They said it wasn't good for me to give in to my fears. They didn't want to spoil me. That was a big thing with them. Because we had a lot of money and servants, they were afraid I would be spoiled. I wasn't supposed to do any work like washing the dishes or shoveling the snow. We had servants for that. I was supposed to grow up to be a lady and know how to manage servants. So, in order to keep me from being spoiled, they sent me to a tough private school where I had a lot of homework. Besides that, I had to take dancing lessons and piano and horseback riding and tennis and flower arranging and watercolor painting. I was supposed to be cultivated. I was always taking something. Every afternoon after school there would be lessons of some kind, and I had all that homework, too. We had a subscription to the Boston Symphony and I had to go every Sunday, and after that we called on people and I had to learn how to make conversation with them and drink tea without spilling any on my lap. You know, in the end I envied the servants, for they were free to do what they wanted once they got their work done. My work was never done. Then J. P. came along, and I learned what a terrible life I'd been lead-ing. I learned that there was such a thing as having fun. What was the use of having all that money if I never could do anything I wanted?"

Well, it sounded pretty good to me, but I didn't say so. Instead, I said, "What did your parents think when you ran away with J. P.?"

"Oh, they were amazed and horrified. They couldn't understand it. I was only sixteen, remember. They had no use for J. P. They thought he was a bum. They sent the cops after me, and the cops brought me home. I ran away again the next day, and that time they let me go. I guess they thought I would get it out of my system and come creeping home in a little while. But I never did.''

"Did you ever tell them you and J. P. got married?''

"No,'' she said. "I haven't laid eyes on them since.''

"They don't know about me and Ooma?''

"J. P. thought that would be a bad idea. He thought they might try to take you two away from us.''

Ooma was sitting with her chin propped up in her hands. "I wish we could go visit them,'' she said. "I wish we could sit on the porch and eat strawberry ice cream with those funny spoons.''

"How about laying off that stuff, Gussie?'' J. P. said. "You're putting all kinds of ideas in their heads.''

"I think they ought to know something about their grandparents,'' Gussie said. "It's hard enough that they can't ever see them.''

"You father had me jailed, remember, Gussie?'' J. P. said.

"J. P., if I decide I want to see my parents sometime, I'm going to do it,'' Gussie said.

"Over my dead body,'' he said. "That man had me jailed. As far as I'm concerned, he's the enemy.''

"I'm going to make my own decision about that,'' she said.

"We'll talk about it later,'' he said, looking pretty grim. It seemed like for Gussie that stealing the motor home was kind of the last straw. It had really got her sore at J. P., and I figured something might come out of it. But I wasn't going to take a chance on that. J. P. had a way of getting people to do what he wanted, and there was no telling what Gussie might do.

I was bound and determined that I was going to see my grandparents, though, so I waited for my chance until I could talk to Gussie alone. A couple of days later we were camped in a field somewhere. J. P. was working on the other van with the Wiz and Trotsky, and Ooma was watching—she liked to listen to J. P. swear when he was working on something. Gussie was cooking supper. I came over to her and said, "Do you think we'll ever see our grandparents?"

She turned around and looked at me. For a minute she didn't say anything. Then she said, "Fergy, you'll be grown-up in a few years. Then you can do anything you want."

"Maybe they'll be dead by then," I said.

"I don't think so," she said. "Your grandfather is only sixty-two. He's likely to live a long time yet."

"Do you think they still live in the same place?" I said.

She went on looking at me. "Why do you ask that, Fergy?"

"Well, I mean when I'm a grown-up, if I want to go visit them."

"Oh," she said. "I see. Yes. The house has been in my mother's family for four generations. She would never sell it."

"They would be pretty surprised, I guess," I said. "I mean, seeing as they don't even know they have grandchildren."

She didn't say anything for a minute. Then she said, "They know. Every once in a while I write them a letter. Just so they know I'm still alive. It would be just too hard for them if I didn't. But I've never told J. P. I just write them a little bit about how everybody is. They know about you and Ooma. I don't do everything the way J. P. wants."

"Do they ever write back?"

"No. How could—" But then we heard J. P. and Ooma coming back, and we had to change the subject.

Ooma was pretty curious about her grandparents, that was clear, and suddenly I decided I ought to take her with me when I ran away. She was headed for trouble. She'd got so much in the habit of stealing that she didn't see anything wrong with it and did it all the time. And if she didn't go to school and learn to read and write and add and subtract and all the rest of it, by the time she grew up she wouldn't know anything at all. She wouldn't be able to get a job, and she'd have to steal to earn her living. Sooner or later, she was bound to get caught stealing something big and go to jail for it.

So I ought to take her with me. She wouldn't like going to school or living in a regular house. She liked being dirty and traveling around in a van. But I figured I ought to take her for her own good, if I could talk her into it.

To tell the truth, there was more to it than that. The idea of running away by myself and hitching from Kansas or someplace all the way back to Cambridge, Massachusetts, without any money was kind of scary. I knew I'd feel a lot better if Ooma came along. She'd be company for me.

But first I had to talk her into doing it. It was a couple of days before I had the chance. By that time, we'd got out to Arkansas and were camped way out in the country on a dirt road that ran through some woods. The woods ran down into a little valley. There was a stream at the bottom. The dirt road stopped there. Across was just more woods. As soon as we got camped that afternoon, I walked down there with a bucket to get some water. It was pretty down there, with the sun shining on the water, making it sparkle, and the birds peeping and chattering in the trees. I squatted down to look for fish. A trout sat in the little pool, keeping itself still in the water by flicking its tail a little. I brought the water back up and said to Ooma, "There's some fish in the stream down there. Come on, I'll show them to you."

71

Ooma liked it when I paid attention to her, because I was her big brother, so she was glad to come. We walked on down the dirt road through the woods to the stream. I crouched down and she crouched down beside me, and we squatted there for a while watching the trout. Then Ooma got bored and got a stick and tried to poke the trout with the stick to see what it would do. But, of course, it darted away the minute the stick touched the water.

"Damn it," she said.

"You can't catch a trout with a stick," I said. "They're too skittish."

She threw the stick into the water and watched it float downstream. Then she sat down and began to take off her ratty old sneakers. Her feet were filthy. "I'm going in there and stand still and see if it'll come to me."

"It won't," I said. "The water's going to be cold."

"I don't care," she said.

"Boy, your feet are dirty," I said.

"None of your damn business," she said.

I didn't say anything. She finished taking off her shoes. Then I said, "It'd be pretty interesting to see what Gussie's old house looks like. I mean, all that fancy silverware and the gardens. I bet they have a Rolls-Royce."

"Or a Mercedes."

"I wish we could visit them and find out."

"Gussie would never let us," Ooma said. "She hates them."

Suddenly I didn't think that was so. I didn't have any reason for thinking that; it was just a feeling I had. "She doesn't hate them, Ooma. She just couldn't get along with them when she was a kid."

"How come she never goes to see them?"

"J. P. won't let her. I think she would take us to see them if J. P. would let her."

"I'm going to ask her," Ooma said.

"You better not," I said. "J. P. will get sore at you."

She got up and walked into the stream. "Damn," she said.

"I told you it would be cold—a mountain stream at this time of year."

"I didn't think it would be that cold." Still, she stepped out into the middle and stood there looking around for the trout.

I lay back on the ground, with my hands under my head, staring up at the sky through the trees. "Maybe we could go there by ourselves sometime," I said.

"Go where?" she said. "This damn water is sure cold."

"Go to Cambridge and visit our grandparents."

She skipped out of the water and sat down next to me. "I thought you said J. P. would never let us."

"What if we didn't tell them? What if we just took off?" I looked at her to see what she was thinking.

"How far away is it?"

Ooma never looked at maps, and she didn't know where anyplace was, or how far it was to anyplace. Half the time she didn't even know what state we were in. "It isn't too far," I said.

"How would we get there?"

"We could hitchhike."

She put her thumb in her mouth. "I wish we'd gone to live with Mr. and Mrs. Clappers," she said.

That surprised me. I thought she'd completely forgotten about them.

"Me, too," I said. "But J. P. and Gussie would never have let us."

"What if we just took off the way you said and hitched?"

"I don't know if Mr. and Mrs. Clappers even like us anymore," I said.

She took the thumb out of her mouth. "Why not? Mrs. Clappers said I was pretty if I would wash my face and fix up my hair."

I sat up. I was beginning to get an idea. "Ooma, they probably think we helped J. P. steal their motor home."

"Why would they think that? We didn't steal it."

"They probably think we made friends with them just to get them away from the motor home so J. P. could steal it. I don't think they would like us anymore."

She stared at me. "Yes, they do like me," she shouted.

"I'm not so sure," I said.

She jumped to her feet. "That's a damn lie," she shouted. "I'll kill you for saying that. Mrs. Clappers likes me, she likes me."

"Calm—"

I was still sitting and she was standing. She jumped on me, clutching her arms around my head and squeezing. I staggered up and pulled her loose. She swung at me with her fingernails. I grabbed her arms and held her away from me. She kicked out at my legs, but I was able to dance back, still holding her. "Calm down, Ooma," I said. "Okay, we'll go and find them. We'll find them and see if they like us or not." But we would head for Cambridge instead.

NINE

WHAT WERE THEY LIKE, I wondered? It seemed like from what Gussie said they might be strict. But maybe they would be kind, too. I tried to imagine what they looked like. I figured they must have white hair, or gray hair, at least. I figured they must have really nice clothes, too. But that's about all I could imagine. How would I find them? I knew my grandfather's name was Gordon E. Hamilton and I could look up his address in the Cambridge phone book, if he was still living there. Then what would I do—just go to the house and knock on their door? What would I say when they answered? It was clear that I had a lot of things to think over.

I began by working out a careful plan for getting away. We'd have to sneak out of the motor home around three in the morning, a couple of hours before daylight. We'd steal J. P.'s money and a couple of maps. For once I didn't mind stealing: After all the stealing J. P. had done, he deserved to have something stolen from him. Then we'd sneak away. They wouldn't think much of it if they heard us going outside. We had a chemical toilet in the motor home, but we were used to going outside and did it most of the time, anyway, so as not to wake everybody up.

We'd travel as fast as we could, walking. In two hours at night, we'd be able to cover six or seven miles. Whenever we heard a car coming we'd duck into the woods, if there were any, or lie flat in a field. They wouldn't know which direction we'd gone in, or whether we'd turned off at some crossroads, and it would take them a lot of time to cover all the roads around there. By that time, I figured, we'd have been able to hitch a ride to get away from that area, and after that they'd never catch us. They might think we'd headed for California or down South or something.

Now that I had got Ooma into it, I was eager to get going. But we had a couple of days of rain, so I waited. Every night I watched the news on TV—we could get only one channel out there—to see what the weather was going to be like. Finally we got a weather report saying it was going to be clear for a few days, and I knew we should go that night.

I wanted to take some extra clothes if we could. You always should look respectable when you're hitchhiking, and if we were ducking around the woods or lying down in fields we'd want to be able to change. But Ooma hardly had any extra clothes, and I didn't have very many. I also wished I could have washed Ooma up a little, but it would have looked pretty suspicious if I had.

So I waited until Gussie had gone down to the stream to wash some clothes, and J. P. and the Wiz were doing something to the engine of the van, and I snuck a clean shirt each for me and Ooma, and a couple of maps out of the motor home. I took them up the dirt road a ways and hid them in the woods. I put a stick on the ground by the edge of the dirt road, pointing in the direction of where I'd hidden the stuff.

The next thing was the money. J. P. always kept all our money in his wallet, and he carried his wallet in the hip pocket of his jeans. At night he laid his jeans on the floor by his bunk. He said he used to hang them over the steering wheel of the van at night, but a long time ago somebody reached into the window and stole his wallet, pants and all, so now he kept his pants close to him at night. It was going to be tricky getting hold of the wallet, but we'd need at least some money for food. I didn't know how long it would take us to get to Cambridge: It was about fifteen hundred miles, and if we had luck and got long rides from truckers and such, we could make it in two or three days; if we didn't have luck, it could take us a week. That would be a long time to go without food. I knew about stuff like that because J. P. was always telling us stories about when he used to hitch a lot before he went onto the old commune.

I didn't want to tell Ooma until the last minute that we were going to run away that night, for fear she'd say something; but then, as we were getting ready for bed, I took her aside and told her. She put her thumb in her mouth and got quiet, but she was willing. I felt a little bad about fooling her this way, but I told myself it was all for the good, and once she met our grandparents she'd like them better than she liked Mr. and Mrs. Clappers.

We went to bed. The big problem was keeping myself awake. We all usually went to bed at the same time—you hardly could do anything else, living the way we did. J. P. turned off the lights, and I lay there staring out into the dark, trying not to fall asleep. First, I made myself name all the states. But every time I'd get thirty or so of them done, I'd forget which ones I'd named and would have to go back over them. Then all at once I jerked awake and realized I'd fallen asleep.

I eased myself up onto my elbows and looked through the darkness at the digital clock built into the stove. It was only eleven-thirty. I lay back down and started going over the times tables. I'd learned the easy ones that time I'd gone to school. Later on, I'd figured out the rest of them by adding, made a chart of them, and learned them. But there were some I kept forgetting. I never could remember what seven times eight was—whether it was fifty-six or sixty-two. So I lay there in the dark saying the times tables to myself and figuring out the ones I couldn't remember, and all at once I woke up again. It was half past four. We should already have been gone because it was going to start getting light soon.

I sat up in bed and listened through the dark. I could hear J. P. snore a couple of times the way he did, and I could hear Ooma breathing because she was right next to me. I couldn't hear Gussie. I just had to chance it that she was asleep.

Moving as quiet as I could, I slid out of bed, dropped down onto my hands and knees, and began to crawl in the direction of J. P.'s bed. It was pitch dark down there on the floor. I kept waving my hand in front of my face so I wouldn't bump into the table or knock down a chair. Finally, I could hear J. P. breathe and I knew I was right next to his bed. I felt along the floor with my hands. In a minute I found his blue jeans. I patted them here and there, until I touched a lump. I reached into the pocket and slid the wallet out. I put the wallet into my own hip pocket. It felt funny having it there, like a part of J. P. was on me.

Then I turned around and crawled back along the floor in the other direction to where Ooma's bunk was. J. P. gave another snore in the dark. I felt around in front of me and found Ooma's bunk. I raised up on my knees, put my hand over Ooma's mouth, and gave her a little shake.

"Umm," she said suddenly, through my hand.

"Shush," I whispered.

She grabbed my hand. She was still only half-awake and didn't know what was going on. "Lummm," she said.

"Shush." She didn't say anything. I took my hand off her mouth. "Let's go," I whispered.

78

Then Gussie said in a low voice, "Is that you, Fergy?"
I jumped. "I'm just going outside," I whispered.

She didn't say anything. I figured she was only half-awake, too. I took Ooma's hand and helped her slide out of bed. Then I put her in front of me, sort of carrying her so that Gussie wouldn't see in the faint light that it was two of us. I tiptoed to the door, set Ooma down, eased the door open, and we slipped out into the night. I just wished that Gussie hadn't woken up, because if she was awake after a while she would start wondering what was taking me so long.

It was chilly. There was no moon, but the sky was clear and there was a good deal of starlight. I took the wallet out of my pocket and felt around inside for the money. I put the money in my back pocket. Then I set the wallet down near the back steps, where they wouldn't see it right away, but would find it when they started looking for it.

"I'm cold," Ooma said.

"Shush," I said. I took her hand, and we tiptoed up the dirt road to where I had left the stick marker. I went into the woods and got the extra shirts and the maps. Then we ran on up to the end of the dirt road.

Up here was a blacktop road going east and west. East was where we wanted to go. We stopped for a minute to catch our breaths, and I stood there listening for sounds and looking back down the dirt road, kind of silver in the starlight. I didn't hear or see anybody, so we began to jog along the blacktop road. We went on for half an hour, jogging a ways and then walking to catch our breaths, and then jogging again. We couldn't run too fast, because Ooma wanted to hold my hand. A couple of times we saw headlights around a bend behind us, and we ducked off into the woods and lay in the dead leaves until the cars went by.

Then it began to get light. I figured it must be after

five. Gussie and J. P. usually got up between six and seven. They'd be up in an hour or so. Once they were up, they'd come after us right away. I hoped they wouldn't think we were kidnapped. At least I hoped Gussie wouldn't worry about us too much. I didn't care what J. P. thought.

The main thing was to get a ride before they came after us. But there wasn't much traffic on that road. Once a truck came along. There was a load of pigs in the back and two people in the front. The woman in the passenger seat gave us a long look, putting her head out of the window and looking back at us after they passed. I hoped people weren't going to think it was funny to see a couple of kids hitchhiking by themselves. Another car came along, but it just shot by. We walked and jogged, and time passed, and the sky got lighter and lighter. I wished we would come to a crossroads, so as to throw them off. They were bound to be after us soon. Now I was walking with my head turned backward practically the whole time. All they needed was a glimpse as they came around a corner and they'd know it was us.

Then I began to see the sun coming up through the woods ahead of us, bits and pieces of it shining like red splashes through the trees. "Ooma, we better get into the woods and hide. They're bound to come along soon." We ducked off into the woods and lay there on the dead leaves among the trees, watching the road. Sure enough, in about ten minutes the motor home shot by, going fast. I got a look at Gussie's face. She was staring straight ahead, mighty grim.

"There they go," Ooma said.

"They'll be coming back the other way pretty soon. They'll go along five or ten miles and then, when they don't see us, they'll figure we must have gone in the other direction or be on some other road."

"Are you scared, Fergy?" she said.

"No," I said. I was, but I didn't want her to know.

"I'm scared," she said. "I didn't know running away would be so scary."

"You don't need to be scared," I said. "I'm right here."

"Still, I'm scared."

We sat there in the woods, waiting, and about twenty minutes later the motor home came back the other way. It was going slow this time, and J. P. had his head out the window and was looking out into the woods as he drove along. We ducked low, and the motor home went by.

"Why were they going slow?" Ooma said.

"I figure they must have gone off west first. They would have driven for maybe ten miles and covered the crossroads, if there were any. Then they came back this way. They didn't see us anywhere, and they figured we might be hiding in the woods."

"Will they come searching for us?"

"I figure they're going back to where we were camping to see if we've turned up—you know, just went for a walk or something. Then they won't know what to do. They can't go driving all over the place looking for us, because they're going to get low on gas, and they don't have any money. They can't go too far away from where they're camped, in case we come back. So if we can get a ride pretty soon, I think we'll be safe."

"Do you think they're sorry we ran away? Do you think they're sad?"

"Sure, they're sorry," I said. "I don't care. They shouldn't have stolen that motor home from Mr. and Mrs. Clappers."

"It wasn't Gussie's fault," Ooma said.

I didn't understand that. "What do you mean?"

"She told J. P. to give it back to Mr. and Mrs. Clappers. I heard her."

"When?" I said. "When did she say that?"

"Before," Ooma said.

"Yesterday? A couple of days ago?"

"Before that," she said. "Back when we were camped some other place. You were somewhere—I forget. She had a fight with J. P. about it. She said we shouldn't have taken it, and we ought to give it back."

It seemed like Gussie was going against J. P. a lot these days. I wondered if she didn't believe in him anymore, either. But I was still determined to run away. "Well, they shouldn't have taken it, is all," I said.

"I hope she isn't too sad that we ran away," Ooma said.

"Oh, when we get someplace we'll write them a letter saying we're all right."

That satisfied her. We stood up and came out of the woods and began walking again, and in about ten minutes we got a ride in a truck. There was a man and a couple of kids in the front, and some sacks of onions in the back. "Where y'all going?" the man asked.

"Whitesville," I said, naming a town farther along that I'd got from the map.

"If you don't mind riding with them onions, I'll take you there." We climbed into the back of the truck and sat there on the sacks of onions. The truck was beat-up and going slow, and it worried me that the motor home would suddenly come shooting up on us.

It took us a half hour to get into Whitesville. It wasn't much of a town. They parked in front of a market, and we got out of the truck, thanked them, and walked off like we knew where we were going. When we were out of sight, I looked at the map. I decided we ought to head for Memphis and pick up Highway 40 there. If we got onto a main highway, there was a chance of getting a ride with a long-distance trucker.

We walked through the town to be sure we didn't run

into the onion truck again, and in five minutes we got another ride. This time it was a new Buick four-door. We climbed into the back. The driver was getting bald and wearing a business suit. He turned around to look at us. "Where you heading for?"

"Memphis," I said.

He turned back to the road and started up. "That's a pretty fair trip for a couple of kids."

"I'm fourteen," I said. "I hitchhike a lot. It's normal for me."

"Oh?" he said. "You live in Memphis?"

"Yes," I said. "We were visiting my aunt back there in Whitesville. We were supposed to come home by bus, but I lost the tickets."

"Why didn't your aunt drive you in?"

I didn't like the way this guy was asking so many questions. "Her car wouldn't start."

"Wouldn't your dad come to get you if you called up? I'll bet he would. It'd be a lot safer than hitchhiking."

I was beginning to sweat a little. "I was scared to tell him I lost the bus tickets. He'd give me hell. He's pretty tough, my old man."

"I see," the guy said. He drove on for a while, fiddling with the radio, which was a relief, because it stopped him from asking questions. But after a half hour he got bored with the radio and turned it off. "Where'd you kids say you were going in Memphis?"

I was in trouble again, because I didn't know the name of a single street there. "You probably wouldn't know of it," I said. "It's just a little street."

"Oh, I might know it," he said. "I've lived in Memphis all my life."

"Oh," I said.

"If you tell me the name I'll drop you off."

"That's all right," I said. "We can take a bus." I figured a town that big had to have a bus.

"No trouble. Where is it?"

I was beginning to sweat all over again. "Well, see, the thing is, I don't want my old man to see us drive up in a car, when we were supposed to take the bus. He'll know something's fishy."

"Oh, I get it," the man said. "Well, I could drop you nearby. We wouldn't have to go right to the house."

I felt hot and scratchy, and the sweat was really sliding down my face. I'd never done much lying and wasn't used to it. Ooma was looking out the window, paying no attention to the trouble I was in. "Well, see, he might be out at the store or something and see us. He might be walking around. It would be better if you dropped us off in some main place and we took a bus home."

"Okay, fine," he said.

I took my handkerchief and wiped the sweat off my face. Ooma stopped looking out the window. "How long will it take to get there?" she said.

I kicked her leg. "The same as always," I said. I kicked her again.

"Oh," she said.

The driver chuckled, but he didn't say anything. We drove on, and about a half hour later he stopped for gas. We got out and went to the bathrooms. I had a feeling that it would be a good idea to get away from this guy, but I didn't know how to do it. I couldn't just explain that we'd changed our minds about going to Memphis and that we were going to hang around the gas station for a while. I kind of hoped he was tired of us and would just drive away.

But when we came back from the toilets, the Buick was standing by the pumps. The guy was inside the gas station making a phone call. He finished, hung up, and came out again. "You kids like a soda?" he said.

"Sure," Ooma said. There was something that worried me about that, but I couldn't figure out what.

"Say thank you, Ooma."

"That's her name? Ooma?"

"It means filled with sweetness and light," Ooma said.

"Oh," the guy said. "What's your name, son?"

"Fergy. That's short for Fergus."

"Does it mean something?" He certainly wasn't in any hurry to get going again.

"No," I said. "It's just a name."

"Oh. What kind of sodas do you kids like?"

"Sprite," Ooma said.

"What about you, Fergus?"

"I'll take a Pepsi. Please. Say please, Ooma."

"Please."

The guy reached into his pocket for his change and strolled back into the gas station. I watched him through the big front window. First, he poked around in the change in his hand to see if he had enough for the machine. Then, he put the change back in his pocket, took out his wallet, and strolled into the back part of the garage where the guy who pumped the gas was looking inside the motor of a Dodge. He stood talking to the gas station man for a little while. Finally, the gas station guy picked up a rag off the fender of the car and began wiping his hands.

Suddenly I got it. He'd called the cops on us and was stalling around until they came.

TEN

I GRABBED OOMA'S HAND. "Come on," I said. "We got to get out of here."

"What?" she said. "He's getting us sodas."

I yanked her arm. "Come on, he called the cops. Let's go." Ooma had always been pretty scared of cops. We started to run together. We took off around the side of the gas station, headed out back. Just as we rounded the corner, I heard the guy from the Buick shout, "Hey. Hey, you kids."

We ran around back of the gas station. There was a big empty field behind it, a potato field or something. Beyond the field there was some kind of a woods. I let go of Ooma's hand, and we started racing across the field toward the woods, Ooma trying to keep up with me and shouting, "Wait up, Fergy, wait up."

Behind us I heard another shout: "Hey, you kids. Come on back here."

I slowed down so Ooma could catch up and looked back. The guy from the Buick and the gas station guy were standing behind the gas station at the edge of the field looking at us. Just then, I heard a police siren whine a little, and a police car slid into the gas station. Ooma caught up and grabbed my shirt. "Are they going to catch us?"

"Come on, let's go." We ran on. The woods were closer. I slowed down again to let Ooma catch up. Two cops were standing at the edge of the potato field with the guy from the Buick and the gas station guy. "Hey, you kids," one of them shouted. Ooma caught up and we went on running. Then we dashed into the woods. We pushed on through the brush until we were a good ways inside. We stopped and stood there sweating and panting and trying to catch our breaths.

"Maybe we shouldn't have run away, Fergy," Ooma said. "Maybe we should go back to J. P. and Gussie."

"We'll be all right, Ooma," I said. But I wasn't sure we would be. I looked back through the trees and across the potato field to the gas station. The gas station guy was gone, but the two cops and the guy from the Buick were standing there. I looked around. If the woods were big enough, they would have a hard time finding us in them, and we could go through them and come out on some road a long ways from the gas station. But if they weren't very big, the cops could drive around to the other side and wait for us to come out. They might even send hound dogs in after us. I'd seen that on TV, where they give the hound dogs something of yours to smell, and then they come after you, barking and howling and following your scent. I wondered if we'd dropped anything in the car. I wondered if they could pick up our scent from the car seat.

Anyway, we had to get out of there. I took a look at the sun so as to get a direction, and we started pushing our way through the woods. It was pretty tough going. The brush was wiry and snapped in our faces and scratched us. About every five minutes, I had to stop to let Ooma rest. She was pretty scratched up and scared and unhappy, and I knew that if I didn't cheer her up pretty soon she was going to quit and go back to J. P. and Gussie. We pushed on; and in about ten minutes I began to see light through the trees ahead. The woods were coming to an end.

"You sit down here, Ooma," I said. "I'm going to check it out ahead."

"I want to come with you," she said.

I looked at her. She was trying not to cry, but tears were leaking out of her eyes. "Okay, come on," I said. We eased through the woods, going carefully this time, and in a couple of minutes we came near the edge. "Wait here," I said. I dropped flat, crawled to the edge, and looked out through the brush. Ten feet away was an old dirt farm road, and across it another open field, stretching as far as I could see to some hills way in the distance. I slid the top half of my body out of the woods partway onto the dirt road and took a look down it. The cop car was coming slowly toward me. I slid back into the woods. "The cops are coming, Ooma," I said. "Quick."

We pushed our way back into the woods about fifty feet and dropped flat. One good thing about all that brush was that the cops wouldn't be able to see through it very well. We lay there waiting, and in a minute, through the brush, I could see bits and pieces of the cop car easing along the dirt road. It stopped. I could see a piece of the car window and part of a cop's head sticking out of it. "They must be in there somewhere, Joe."

I couldn't hear what Joe said back. The first cop said, "Well, I ain't goin' in there after them. I got on good pants." Joe said something more, which I couldn't hear, and the first cop said, "Forget it, Joe. We'll catch up with them sooner or later. They won't be hard to spot." Then the cop car started up again and slid out of sight.

"They won't catch us, will they, Fergy?"

"No," I said. But we were going to be pretty obvious hitchhiking around there.

"I'm hungry," Ooma said.

"I wish I had a watch," I said. I'd always wanted a watch, but J. P. would never buy me one. He said I shouldn't get uptight about time. But he had a watch.

"I'll steal you a watch, Fergy," Ooma said.

"No, don't do that, Ooma."

"I want to," she said.

"Don't," I said. All I needed was for Ooma to get caught stealing something. I looked up at the sun. It was around eleven o'clock, I figured. "It isn't lunchtime yet," I said. "We'll get something to eat pretty soon." I pushed my way back to the edge of the woods. There was brown dust in the air, and the cop car was turning around in the field. I slid back into the woods a little ways. After a bit, the cop car rumbled past. I waited until it was gone, leaving more brown dust in the air behind it. Then we came out of the woods and started to walk off down the dirt road, the woods on one side of us, the big field on the other, heading I didn't know where.

"When are we going to eat, Fergy?"

I was pretty hungry myself. We hadn't had any breakfast. "Pretty soon," I said. "As soon as we get someplace."

We walked on, and after a little while I saw a farm up ahead—a house, a barn, a couple of sheds, a chicken house. I stopped and thought about it. Would the cops have put out some kind of report about us on the radio? I didn't think we were important enough for that. I looked at the farm a little more, trying to get some idea of it. It seemed kind of ramshackle. The paint was peeling off the house, and the barns and sheds were gray. There was an old farm truck parked in front of the barn. I wondered if they would give us a ride to some town.

"Maybe they'll give us something to eat," Ooma said. "Maybe they have hamburgers and potato salad."

"Don't get your hopes up," I said.

We walked on up to the farm. It was beat-up, all right. There was a porch across the front of the house, with half the slats broken out of the railing. An old swinging bench was hanging by rusty chains from the porch ceiling. A couple of little kids were playing on the swinging bench, and a rooster was sitting up on the back, enjoying the ride. We stood at the bottom of the porch. The two little kids stared at us. They both had jeans on and long, tangled hair, and I couldn't tell if they were girls or boys. The rooster began to crow and flap its wings. "Are your folks at home?" I said.

They stared at us some more. One of them shook its head. "Yes, they are too," the other one said. Its hair was longer and it seemed like a girl.

Ooma went up on the porch. "Ask your mom if we can have something to eat."

"Ooma, cut that out," I said.

Ooma sat down on the bench and began to swing it back and forth. "This is pretty neat," she said. The rooster began to squawk and hopped off.

Just then, a woman opened the front door and looked out. She was wearing jeans and a dirty T-shirt and was pretty thin. "I thought I heard somebody," she said. "Where'd y'all come from?"

"We're hun—" Ooma said.

"We got lost," I said. "We were trying to take a shortcut through the woods, and we got lost."

She looked at us and tucked in her T-shirt. "Where y'all heading for?"

I decided to stay away from Memphis this time. It had got the guy in the Buick suspicious because it was too far for a couple of kids to be hitching to. "Janesboro," I said, which was another town I'd got off the map. "We were visiting my aunt over at Whitesville and we started hitching back, but I decided to take a

90

shortcut and now we don't know where we are." I was beginning to get pretty good at telling lies.

"Can we have something to eat?"

"Ooma, cut that out." I looked at the woman. "She doesn't have good manners. She always says anything she wants to."

The woman laughed. "Well, I guess I can spare something. Come on in." So we followed her into the house, her kids coming along behind us, and out back to the kitchen. It was as ramshackle as the house—an old, beat-up enamel table, a gas stove, an old icebox with the white chipped off in places, like someone had whacked at it with a hammer. She sat us down and fixed us peanut-butter-and-jelly sandwiches. We all sat there at the enamel table—us, the little kids, the woman—eating peanut-butter sandwiches and drinking Coke. After a while, the farmer came in, and I told him all my lies about getting lost by taking a shortcut from Whitesville to Janesboro.

"You're a long way from the Janesboro road," he said.

"Well, I know it now," I said. "I got mixed up."

He gave me a look. "You live over in Janesboro?"

"Yes," I said. I sure hoped he wasn't going to ask me where, for I didn't know any more about Janesboro than I did about Memphis. To get him off the subject of Janesboro, I said, "We were visiting my aunt over in Whitesville."

It didn't work. "Where'd you say you lived over in Janesboro?"

I hadn't said where we lived, but it wouldn't do any good to say so. "In the center of town," I said.

"Oh?" he said. "I'm going over there in the truck after a little while to pick up a load of chicken feed. I could drop you off."

That was all to the good, for it would get us away

from the cops who were looking for us. "We sure would be glad of a ride," I said.

"What kind of truck do you have?" Ooma said.

"Ooma, don't—"

"A Ford three-quarter ton," he said.

"We got a big motor home," Ooma said. "It has TV and everything."

The farmer squinted at us. "I thought you said you lived in Janesboro."

I stepped on Ooma's foot under the table. "See, that's the thing," I said. "We're supposed to meet our folks in the center of Janesboro. They're going to get there this afternoon."

The farmer looked at Ooma, and then me. "I don't get it," he said. "Where are they now?"

I was beginning to sweat and feel red. I could see that I still needed a lot of practice at lying. "Well, see, they left us off in Janesboro to visit—"

"I thought you said Whitesville," the woman said.

"I mean Whitesville." I wiped some sweat off my upper lip. "See, they dropped us off in Whitesville to visit our aunt and said they'd meet us in Whitesville."

"Don't you mean Janesboro?" the farmer said.

"I mean Janesboro."

"How come your folks didn't come back to your aunt's to pick you up?"

I wiped some sweat off my forehead with my sleeve. "See, the thing is, my dad doesn't get along with my aunt so hot. He just dropped us off." I had to get away from them. "Listen, could I use your bathroom?"

So they told me where it was, and I left and splashed some water on my face to cool myself down; and when I came back Ooma was outside on the porch swinging the little kids and the rooster; and after about an hour we climbed into the back of the truck and headed off for Janesboro.

I was feeling pretty nervous. The farmer didn't believe much of my story, and I worried that he'd drive us right to the police station or something. I was thinking about this, when Ooma nudged me. "Look, Fergy," she said. She held out her hand. In it was a watch.

I snatched it up. "Where'd you get that?" I said.

"From them. It's a present."

"Ooma, for—" Then I stopped. Her eyes were shining and she was looking at me, so pleased and happy she'd got me something I wanted. I just didn't have the heart to bawl her out. "Well, thanks," I said. "Thanks a lot."

"It's a present," she said, looking happy. It must have been lying around on a table somewhere in the house, and she'd grabbed it up when she'd gone out to the porch to swing those little kids. Now what was I going to do? The right thing would be to leave it in the back of the truck when we got out, so that the farmer would think it had fallen off his wrist sometime. But, of course, Ooma would be pretty quick to realize I didn't have it anymore. I'd have to tell her I'd given it back, and her feelings would be hurt. I didn't know what to do, so I stuck the watch in my pocket and decided to think about it some more. Ooma put her head over the side of the truck so she could catch the air on her face, until I told her to bring her head back before she got it hit on something. We went along for half an hour, and then we saw a sign saying JANESBORO. We drove into the town past the usual gas stations and stores and all of that, until we came to a shopping mall. It was just like all the rest I'd been in—a supermarket, a dry cleaners, a big drugstore, a Sears. The farmer pulled his truck into the middle of the mall and parked it among the other cars. He opened the door and got out. "This is as far as I go," he said. He gave me a squinty look. "Sure you kids'll be okay?"

"Our dad will be along pretty soon," I said.

I stood up in the truck and so did Ooma. Then she said, "Look, Fergy." She pointed over the cab of the truck. I looked. There was the motor home parked in front of the drugstore. The folding table was set up, and J. P. was standing beside it giving his talk. Gussie was making change, and Trotsky and the Wiz were circulating through the crowd handing out copies of "Extracts from the Journals of J. P. Wheeler."

ELEVEN

THE FARMER WAS looking out toward where Ooma was pointing. "Blamed if I believed a word of it," he said, "but I see it's true."

All I wanted to do was grab Ooma's hand and make a run for it—run on out of that shopping mall, down the main street, and out of Janesboro. But I couldn't—not with that farmer standing there watching us. So I climbed down out of the truck and helped Ooma down. She stood there on the ground with her thumb in her mouth, staring in the direction of the motor home. "Well," I said to the farmer, "thanks a whole lot for giving us a ride. My folks will be glad we made it on time."

"It wasn't anything," the farmer said. He was looking off toward the motor home, too. "What are they all doing?" he asked.

It was nice to be able to tell the truth for a change and not have to worry about getting caught. "They sell stuff," I said. "Honey and things." I decided not to mention the high blood pressure.

"Maybe I'll go over and have a look," he said.

The main thing was, he was curious about us— about Ooma and me turning up at his house, and not having a very good story about how we happened to be there, and all of this business of the motor home. Oh, I could have killed Ooma for opening her mouth about the motor home back there at his farm. Why couldn't she ever keep her mouth shut? Here we'd run a hundred miles to get away from Gussie and J. P., and now we were right back in their laps again.

I grabbed Ooma's hand. "I have to take her to the bathroom," I said. I looked around. The store closest to us was the Sears. "Come on, Ooma."

He gave me a look. "Don't you have a bathroom in that fancy motor home?"

"It's broken," I said. "It doesn't work. Come on, Ooma." I gave her arm a jerk. She almost fell down.

"Fergy—"

I pulled her again. "Come on, Ooma," I said. "Come on before you wet yourself." I began to drag her across the shopping mall toward the Sears.

She slugged my arm with her fist. "Damn it, Fergy." But I went on dragging her, and she went on cursing and shouting and trying to peel my fingers off her wrist. I gave the farmer a quick look. He stared at me, and then he began to trot off in the direction of the folding table. He was going to tell J. P. that he'd just dropped a couple of kids off, that was for sure. I dragged Ooma into the Sears, down one of the aisles, past a stack of chain saws, past a heap of motor oil, through the kids' shoe department, toward the back. "Be good, Ooma," I said, "and I'll let you steal something." She calmed down a little at that, and we went on through the Sears and out the rear doors.

A long loading platform ran along the rear of the store. Backed up to it were four or five big trailer trucks. We stood next to one that said ACME CARPET COMPANY. The rear doors were open, and I could see that it was half-filled with big rolls of carpeting. I looked in the other direction. A wide driveway led out onto the main street of Janesboro. I could see traffic going along the street and some stores opposite. Now what? We had to move fast. We could run down the drive to that main street and beat it out of Janesboro. But I wasn't sure that was the best idea. Once that farmer told J. P. we were in town, he'd come after us like a shot, and the first place he'd look would be out there.

I grabbed Ooma's hand again. "Come on. We've got to get out of here fast."

"Fergy, maybe we shouldn't run away anymore. Maybe we should go back and stay with Gussie and J. P."

I didn't have much time for arguing. "I thought you wanted to find Mr. and Mrs. Clappers," I said. "I thought you wanted to live with them."

She didn't say anything, but put her thumb in her mouth. "Maybe we could just go over and say hello."

"Ooma, we can't do that. If we did, they'd catch us and make us stay."

She went on sucking her thumb. "It was nice in that motor home." It was pretty hard for her to be this close to Gussie and J. P. and not go to see them.

"Listen," I said. "By now Mr. and Mrs. Clappers'll have a new motor home. A brand-new one."

She didn't say anything, but went on sucking her thumb. We had to get going pretty quick. "It will be nice having Mrs. Clappers wash your face and put your hair up every morning, won't it?" That got her a little. "We can always come back to live with J. P. and Gussie if we want to." To Ooma, all places were right near to each other. "Come on, we've got to hurry. They'll start looking for us soon."

Then I happened to look back toward the Sears. Through the glass door, way in the distance among the shoppers and the chain saws and baby shoes, I saw J. P. and Gussie pushing their way through the crowd. They didn't see us yet, but they were headed straight toward the back. "Quick, Ooma, they're coming." I grabbed her hand. Where could we go? If we made a break for it down the driveway they would spot us for sure, because

I wasn't going to be able to go very fast dragging Ooma along behind me.

Then I noticed the carpet truck. "Quick," I said. I picked Ooma up and threw her into it on top of the rolls of carpet. I swung myself in after her and scrambled way into the back, dragging Ooma along behind me. They wouldn't see us way back in the dark behind the rolls of carpet. I just had to pray I could keep Ooma from shouting out.

So we waited, and in half a minute I heard running feet. Then the feet stopped right by the rear of the truck, and I heard J. P. say, "I don't see them anywhere out here."

"Maybe they're still in the store," Gussie said.

"Maybe," J. P. said. "Or maybe they went down that driveway and onto the main street."

"Poor Ooma," Gussie said. At that, I felt Ooma wriggle, and I grabbed hold of her so she couldn't jump up. "She wouldn't have run away on her own."

I realized that Gussie wouldn't have run away on her own, either. "What I can't figure out is how they ended up on that guy's farm," J. P. said.

"Let's just find them, J. P."

"I don't want to run—" Ooma started. I clapped my hand on her mouth. She wriggled, trying to get loose from me.

"Shush," I said.

J. P. said, "Fergy's been sulking for a week. I should have guessed he'd try to pull something. He's gotten awfully rebellious recently. He used to be a nice kid, but he won't listen to anything I say anymore."

"It was because you took that motor home. I told you not to," Gussie said. "That was your big idea."

"Don't start that again, Gussie."

Ooma slammed me in the head hard enough to hurt. "Let go of me, Fergy," she said into my hand.

"Did you hear something?" J. P. said.

I realized I couldn't keep Ooma from going back to them, if she really wanted to. It wasn't right; I was just being selfish. I decided that as soon as Gussie and J. P. left I'd let her go. But I didn't want her giving me away. I rolled over on top of her. "Listen to me, Ooma," I whispered in her ear. "If you'll be quiet I'll let you go in a minute." She went on squirming, and I knew she was going to try to bite my hand. "Please, Ooma, shut up for a minute," I whispered. "I promise I'll let you go, and you can go back to J. P. and Gussie."

She kicked me. Just then I heard a voice outside say, "Excuse me, folks." The rear doors to the truck slammed shut. Suddenly we were in the dark. I heard the sound of a bolt sliding and the snap of a lock. Ooma bit me, and I jerked my hand away from her mouth. "Damn you," I said.

"Help," she shouted. The driver's door opened and closed, and the motor started. I grabbed up the corner of a rug and pulled it over Ooma's head. "Help," she shouted. "I'm in here." But her voice was pretty much muffled under the rug. The truck began to move. I heard the gears shift, and I knew we were picking up speed down the driveway. We stopped at the main street. Then came the sound of shifting again, and I knew we were headed along the main street of Janesboro. I had no idea where we were going, but it was away from J. P.

I let Ooma up from under the rug. "Damn you, Fergy," she shouted.

I was afraid the driver would hear her. "Listen, calm down a minute."

"I'm not going to calm down, you pepperhead."

"If you don't calm down, I'm going to put you under the rug again."

She didn't say anything, but sat there in the dark

breathing hard. "Look," I said, "if you really want to go back to J. P. and Gussie, I'll let you."

"They were right there. It's too late now."

"No, it isn't, I said. "This truck'll stop somewhere soon to make its next delivery. We'll get off there, and I'll take you to a police station and they'll find the motor home and tell J. P. where you are."

"I don't believe you. How will they find it?"

"They'll radio around to the other cops. Some cop is bound to know where they are. We never had any shortage of cops hanging around us, did we?"

She didn't say anything. Then she said, "You better promise."

"I promise," I said. I meant it, too. There wasn't any point in trying to drag her along with me if she was going to fight me the whole time. I knew I ought to, for her own good, but it wouldn't work.

"You better not forget," she said. She was still sore at me, but she quieted down and after a little while she lay down and went to sleep. I sat there on the rolls of rugs in the dark, thinking. I had no idea where the truck was going. It could be taking us west instead of east, and I'd have to start out all over again. The idea of that made me feel pretty gloomy. It had taken us an awful lot of trouble just to come as far as we had. But maybe once I left Ooma off, things might go smoother.

So we went on and on. I began to wonder how long we'd been going, and what time it was, and suddenly I remembered that I still had that watch Ooma had stolen from the farmer in my pocket. I got a shock of guilt: I should have left it in the truck, regardless of Ooma's feelings. But suddenly seeing J. P. in that shopping mall had made me forget all about it. I took it out of my pocket and tried to see it in the dark. Even though I felt guilty about it, it was nice to have a watch. I couldn't see a thing, so I put it back in my pocket. We'd be stopping pretty soon, I figured. I was beginning to feel sleepy, too. We'd had an awful lot of excitement recently. I lay down on the rolls of carpet and fell asleep.

After a while I woke up. I didn't have any idea how long I'd been asleep. Ooma was moving around, like she was beginning to wake up, too. It was sort of cold in there now, and I shivered. Why would it be cold? It was May, and we were still out in Arkansas where it was usually hot that time of year. Was it raining? I listened, but I didn't hear the sound of rain.

Suddenly I realized that it must be night. The temperature dropped a lot at night in that part of the country. We'd slept a lot longer than I'd thought. It would have to be eight, nine o'clock for the temperature to have gone down that much. That kind of worried me. We'd been traveling for four or five hours. A truck could cover an awful lot of mileage in that time. What if we were headed out for California or up to Oregon or Washington?

I heard Ooma moving around. Suddenly she said, "Fergy?" pretty scared.

"I'm right here," I said. I felt for her, so she could take my hand.

"Where are we?"

"In a truck, remember?"

"Oh," she said. "I'm hungry."

"The truck'll probably stop pretty soon." But I wasn't sure of that anymore. What if it was a long-distance truck that would travel all night? But I didn't want to say anything like that to Ooma. "Let's go back to sleep," I said. I unrolled a piece of carpet, and we snuggled down under it. The carpet was kind of stiff for a blanket, but it was pretty cozy and warm under it. After a minute, I heard Ooma breathing regularly. I wasn't sleepy myself, and so I lay there worrying and waiting for the truck to stop. It didn't. It just went on and on, and after a while I realized that we must be on some sort of a superhighway, because we didn't ever stop for anything: If we'd been on an ordinary road, there'd have been red lights and stop signs and intersections. Wherever we were going, we'd come a long way from Janesboro. Finally I went to sleep.

I woke up with a bang in my ears and sunlight pouring into the back of the truck. Ooma woke up at the same time. We both sat up in a hurry, blinking. In the square of daylight at the back of the truck, a young guy with a beard was staring in at us. "What the hell is this?" he said.

We got up and crawled over the rolls of rugs to the rear of the truck. The driver went on staring in at us. "How many of you are there?" he said.

We went on crawling. "Just us," I said.

Ooma yawned. "I'm hungry," she said.

"How'd you get in there?"

We climbed over the carpet and dropped onto the ground. It was broad daylight. As close as I could figure, we'd traveled fifteen, sixteen hours. "Thanks for the lift," I said.

The driver grabbed my arm. "Hold it a sec, brother. You're not going anywhere just yet."

"We didn't steal anything," I said. I remembered the watch and blushed a little. "We got in there by mistake, and you locked us in."

He was pretty suspicious. "Where'd you get in?"

"Janesboro," I said. "When you were parked behind the Sears." I looked around. We were parked behind an old red-brick factory with a sign along the top saying ACME CARPET COMPANY. I could see other factories nearby, and in the distance some big apartment buildings. We were in some kind of big city. "What city is this?"

"Never mind that," the driver said. "I want to know what you were doing in there."

I was beginning to feel pretty nervous. All along, I'd

figured we'd climb out of the truck and off we'd go, but this guy sounded like he was about to call the cops. I didn't want to tell him we were running away. "We just needed a ride, is all."

"Where were you running away from?"

"We're not running away," I said. "We were visiting my aunt, and—"

"Don't give me your aunt," he said. "I've been on the road too long. Where'd you come from? What's your hometown?"

"We don't have any home," I said.

"Yes, we do," Ooma said. "We have a motor home that's almost new, with a TV and a stove and closets and everything."

The guy gave me a look. "That right?"

"Yes," I said. "We weren't trying to steal anything."

He looked at us for a little while. Then he let go of my arm and said, "Okay, I guess you couldn't have swiped a two-hundred-pound roll of carpet. But, if you want my advice, you better go on home. You're too young to be drifting around the country like this. You could get hurt. There are a lot of bad dudes out there who'd take advantage of kids like you. If it was me, I'd go on home. I don't know what your folks did to you to make you run away, but you'd be better off putting up with it for a few years longer. Like I say, there are a lot of bad dudes out there."

"We're not drifting around," I said. "We're going to visit our grandparents. But we still don't know where we are."

He nodded his head. Then he said, "Well, I hope your grandfolks live somewhere around Washington, because that's where you are."

"Washington?" My heart sank. We'd gone in entirely the wrong direction. We were three thousand miles from Cambridge, Massachusetts. "Where is this, Seattle?"

He laughed. "No, not Washington State. Washington, D.C."

TWELVE

WELL, OF COURSE my promise that I'd send her back to J. P. and Gussie wasn't any good anymore. I had to tell her that we were stuck now: The only choice we had was to try to get to Cambridge and find our grandparents. When we got there, I told her, they'd give us strawberry ice cream in ginger ale, and if she still wanted to go back to J. P. and Gussie, they'd be able to send her back because they had lots of money.

Ooma wasn't too happy about any of this, but she was pretty exhausted from everything that had happened and didn't have the energy to start a fight with me. I could see that she wasn't up to hitchhiking up to Cambridge, and I decided we would take a bus, if we had enough money. So we asked the way to the bus station. We had just about enough money for bus tickets, because Ooma could go half-fare. There was a little left over, so we had a big breakfast of hot dogs and Devil Dogs and Pepsi, and then we took the bus up to Boston.

The food had put Ooma in a better spirit, and she liked the idea of zipping along in the bus up above the cars, looking at everything that went by. I knew that if she had a nap on the bus she'd be all right. But I was pretty nervous. What if our grandparents didn't live in that big house anymore? What if they didn't live in Cambridge? What if they were dead? There were an awful lot of things that could go wrong with my plan—that was for sure.

We rode all morning and part of the afternoon straight up to New York. Ooma slept for a good while and woke up feeling more cheerful. I had put the watch on my wrist, and every once in a while I looked at it. It wasn't so much that I wanted to know the time: I just liked looking at it, even though I was still kind of ashamed of myself for keeping it.

We changed buses in New York and rode the rest of the afternoon up to Boston. When we got into the city, it was around six o'clock, just starting to get a little dark. We got off the bus in the Boston bus station. I was still scared, for what if we couldn't find them and had no place to sleep? But I was excited, too, thinking about these people who had never seen us, and maybe we were going to be part of them. What would I say to them? I began to work up a little speech and memorize it.

I didn't dare spend any money on food, because we hardly had any left, but I got Ooma a soda and then went off to the phone booths to find a telephone book. I got the one for Cambridge and turned over the pages to find the name of Gordon E. Hamilton. My fingers were trembling and I felt shaky inside. It took me a while to find the name because I was nervous and passed right over it twice. But then I saw it—Gordon E. Hamilton, 11 Berkeley Street, Cambridge. I didn't know if that was the big house that Gussie'd grown up in, but at least they were still living in Cambridge. Or *he* was, anyway.

I memorized the address and got Ooma, and then we went to the information booth and found out how to take the subway nearest to Berkeley Street. We rode on the subway for a half hour, got out, and asked somebody the way. It was just a short walk, he said, around one corner, down that street, and around another corner. We followed the directions, and then we came to Berkeley Street. I looked down it, feeling funny. It was an awful nice street, with big houses and streetlights— including the same one that shone down on Gussie before I was born. I took a deep breath, grabbed Ooma's hand, and we started down the street. It didn't take a minute to come to their house. I knew it without checking the number, for there was a big porch along the front and lots of gardens here and there on the lawn. We stopped in front by the iron gate in the fence, and as we stood there the streetlight that used to shine in Gussie's window suddenly came on. I figured that was a sign of good luck. "That's the house," I said. "Our grandparents are in there."

"Maybe they'll hate us," Ooma said.

"No, they won't," I said. But how could I be sure? I took another deep breath, opened the gate, and we went up the walk and onto the porch. In the middle of the door, there was a big door knocker with a face like a lion. I knocked three times, good and loud.

We waited. Nothing happened. We waited some more. Then the door opened. A young woman wearing a black dress and a white apron was standing there. She was too young to be our grandmother. I figured she was the maid. "Yes, can I help you?" she said.

After rehearsing my speech for an hour, nothing would come out of my mouth. I coughed to get myself started. "Please tell Mr. and Mrs. Hamilton that their grandchildren are here."

The maid jerked back, and then her mouth opened wide. "Their grandchildren? I don't think they have any grandchildren."

"Yes, they do," I said. "Tell them we're the children of Gussie and J. P. Wheeler."

She shut the door. We waited. Nothing happened. We waited some more. I looked at my watch so as to get some idea of how long we would wait. Then I saw one of the curtains in the window along the porch move a little, and part of a face with gray hair was there. The curtain dropped back in place. "I'm scared," said Ooma. "Let's go."

"No," I said. "They won't hate us."

The door opened partway. A man was standing there. He had gray hair and glasses and was wearing a brown sweater over a shirt and necktie. He looked at us for a minute, not saying anything. We just looked back. Then he said, "Please come in."

"Wipe your feet, Ooma," I whispered.

She was pretty scared of going into such a fancy house, and she wiped her feet carefully on the mat. Then we went into a little hall, where there were a couple of little tables, a fancy mirror, and some pictures of hound dogs chasing foxes over a fence. Our grandfather shut the door. We followed him down the hall into the living room. It was the fanciest living room I'd ever been in. There was a fireplace and big glass doors at the back looking out onto a terrace and gardens; and two sofas with red and gold cloth and ornaments carved into the back; and a couple of Oriental rugs; and little tables and chairs here and there; and on the walls, pictures of old-fashioned-looking people who I figured were our ancestors. I could smell roast beef cooking. I wondered if Ooma and I could really live in a place like this. It was too fancy. I figured I could learn to be fancy, but I wasn't sure Ooma could: She'd want to jump on the sofas and put her feet on the tables.

A woman with white hair in kind of a cloud around her head was sitting on one of the sofas. There was knitting on the cushion beside her and a little glass of something brown on a small table in front of her. The glass sparkled in the light. Beside the glass was a little glass bell. Ooma and I stood in the middle of the room, looking around. Our grandfather stood behind us. Our grandmother didn't move. She didn't say anything. She just looked at us.

"What do you think, Margaret?" our grandfather said.

"I don't know what to think. I'm in a state of shock." She picked up the sparkling glass and sipped from it.

"Do you think the girl resembles Augusta?" he said.

She tipped her head a little. "I think she might," she said. "But we're being rude, Gordon. Our guests have probably had a long trip. Please sit down, children."

I felt pretty funny—excited and nervous, happy to be there but not sure I belonged. "We're kind of dirty," I said.

"Gussie and J. P. let me be dirty," Ooma said.

I wished Ooma knew how to keep her mouth shut, but I didn't say anything. Our grandmother laughed. "That's all right. Why don't you sit on that sofa there, so I can get a look at you? You must understand that we're a bit surprised." She sipped at the glass again. "Have you had your suppers?"

"We had stuff in New York awhile ago."

"You have had a long trip," she said.

"I'm hungry as hell," Ooma said.

"Ooma," I said. "I'm sorry, but she swears."

Our grandmother laughed. Now our grandfather sat down in a big chair and stretched his legs out in front of him in a comfortable way. "They don't sound like criminals," he said.

Our grandmother picked up the little glass bell and rang it. In a minute the maid came in. "There will be two more for dinner, Sheila," she said.

Now our grandfather said, "You must understand we're rather flabbergasted. Tell us all about it. To begin with, what are your names?"

I felt sort of embarrassed. "My name's Fergy. That's short for Fergus. And her name's Ooma."

"It means filled with sweetness and light," Ooma said.

Grandmother laughed again. "It's rather pretty. Are you really filled with sweetness and light, Ooma?"

Ooma looked confused, and I was afraid she was going to say something wrong or curse. But she just nodded and put her thumb in her mouth.

"She's okay," I said, "but sometimes she gets a little wild."

They didn't say anything. Then our grandfather said, "I see. Now tell me, where do you live?"

So I told him about everything—the old commune and J. P.'s journals; and traveling around in the van and selling honey; and how I was worried about growing up dumb and wanting to go to school and be on teams and things; and stealing the motor home; and all the rest of it. All the while, our grandparents listened and nodded and here and there asked little questions to make sure they understood it all; and when I got finished they sat looking at each other.

Our grandfather said, "Ooma, do you remember your mother's birthday?"

"You mean Gussie?"

I knew he was asking to make sure we were really Gussie's children. It worried me, because we didn't know the answer. "We weren't supposed to call them Mom and Dad," I said. "J. P. said that was a power trip."

"All right," he said. "Gussie's birthday."

Ooma gave me a look, still confused. She put her thumb in her mouth and said, "I don't know."

I said, "We're not supposed to have birthdays. J. P. says birthdays are bourgeois. Giving birthday presents is just materialism under the guise of altruism."

"You poor children don't even know your own birthdays?"

"Sure we know them," Ooma said. "We went to some school once and Fergy found out."

When we went to that school, Gussie had to show our birth certificates. I snuck them out of her purse and looked at them. Remembering it, I blushed. "I happened to see our birth certificates."

"You mean, you've never had a birthday party, either of you?" our grandfather said.

"No," I said. "It would be too materialistic."

He said nothing. Then he said, "But you don't know your own moth—Gussie's birthday?"

"No," I said. He was relaxed and his face was smooth, but I knew he was suspicious. What would happen to us if they didn't believe us?

Then our grandmother said, "Perhaps you know her middle name?" She looked at me and at Ooma and back to me. Now I was really worried, because we didn't know that, either. "J. P. didn't like it too much when Gussie talked about being a little girl and all. She was supposed to forget all about you."

"So you don't know her middle name, either?"

"No."

His face was still smooth and relaxed, but he was certain to be pretty suspicious of us now. How could I prove we were her children? I couldn't think of anything. "So you don't know anything about your moth—Gussie's childhood? What kind of things she enjoyed, that sort of thing?"

Ooma took her thumb out of her mouth. "Sure we do," she said. "She used to sit on the porch and eat strawberry ice cream in ginger ale with a funny spoon you could suck through."

Our grandparents looked at each other. "Go on, Ooma," our grandmother said. "What else did she do?"

"She was scared of the dark and cried, and her

110

mother had to come in and hug her so she wouldn't be scared."

They weren't so relaxed now, but were listening to her carefully. "Anything else, Ooma?" our grandfather said.

She looked at me, confused again, and put her thumb in her mouth. I said, "She had to go to the Boston Symphony and learn to drink tea, and she had lots of lessons. Piano lessons and dancing lessons and horseback-riding lessons and—" Suddenly I realized it was pretty insulting of me to be bringing up the things she hated them for. I started to blush. "I mean—"

"That's all right, Fergy," our grandmother said. "We came to realize that we had organized her life too much."

Our grandfather said, "You seem to know quite a lot about her childhood, when you get down to it, Fergy. I thought you said J. P. wouldn't let her talk about her past."

"Well, he didn't want her to, but she did, anyway. Ooma always asked her to tell about it."

"She liked to talk about her childhood, then?" our grandmother said. "She remembered some nice things?"

"Oh, yes," I said. "She sure did. She remembered the silverware gleaming on the table and flowers cut fresh every day. It was all so beautiful, she said. J. P. didn't like it when she talked about that stuff, because it was materialistic, but Ooma liked to hear about it."

"What else pleasant did she remember?"

"The streetlight," Ooma said. "She loved the streetlight because it kept away the dark."

Suddenly, Grandfather laughed. "Margaret, I don't think we need pursue this. I think we have the right children here."

When he said that, I felt happy enough to burst, for I knew they would let us stay, at least for a while. I looked around me at the fancy furniture, the garden out back, the pictures of our ancestors. What would it be like to live here and be rich? I couldn't imagine it; I couldn't get the feeling of it at all.

"Fifteen years," our grandmother said. "It's been fifteen years since we've seen her. Of course, she's written from time to time. We always have had some rough idea of what she was up to. It was always terribly painful for us to have grandchildren growing up and not to be able to see them." She stopped for a minute. Then she said, "Tell me, Fergy, do you think she's happy living the way she is?"

I sat there thinking about that. Was Gussie happy or wasn't she? I remembered times when she sat around with J. P. and Trotsky and the Wiz drinking wine and singing. She seemed happy when she did that. Or sometimes if we were camped out in the woods, she and Ooma would go for long walks and come back with wildflowers and braid necklaces out of them. She seemed happy then. But was she really happy?

"Well," I said, "I guess she must have been once, because she wouldn't have stayed with J. P. all these years if she wasn't. I mean, she believed in J. P.—that he was a great man and someday his journals would be famous. But I don't know if she's so happy anymore. She didn't like it when J. P. and the Wiz stole the motor home."

Our grandmother didn't say anything, and I could tell she was wondering if she could get Gussie to come home again.

"Fergy," our grandfather said, "what do you think about J. P.?"

"J. P.?"

"I mean, do you believe he's a great man?"

"I used to," I said. "Not anymore."

"Yes, he is," Ooma said. "He is, too."

"I'm sure he has many good points, Ooma," our grandmother said.

"So that's why you left, Fergy? Because you decided that your father wasn't a great man?"

I hadn't thought about it that way. I'd thought I'd run away mainly so I could go to school. But now I could see that there was more to it: Once you stop believing in your father, you kind of hate him for not being a great man anymore. He seems like a phony to you, and you don't like him anymore. But I didn't want to say any of that. So I said, "Mostly, it was because I was worried about not going to school. I got tired of being dumb and having to believe a whole lot of stuff I didn't want to believe and worrying about Ooma stealing all the time and—" Suddenly I realized that I shouldn't have mentioned about Ooma's stealing.

"Does Ooma steal?" our grandmother said. "Do you steal, Ooma?"

Ooma gave me a quick look. Then she put her thumb in her mouth and nodded.

"What do you steal, Ooma?" our grandmother said.

She took her thumb out of her mouth. "Whatever I want. Gussie and J. P. let me."

"Is that true, Fergy?"

There wasn't any use in lying about it. "It's kind of a habit. She doesn't think there's anything wrong with it."

Then the maid came in and said that dinner was ready. Our grandparents stood up. "Would you like to wash?" our grandmother said.

"Yes," I said. "Come on, Ooma."

"Why the hell do I have—"

I grabbed her arm and pulled her off the sofa. "Come on," I said. They had a bathroom right there in the downstairs near the dining room. I'd never been in a bathroom so nice and clean and sparkling. It had big fluffy towels and smelled of some kind of sweet soap, and there were pictures of wildflowers on the wall. I wondered if those pictures had been there when Gussie was my age.

"God, it's pretty in here," Ooma said.

"Now, you wash up good," I said. "And from now on, cut out the swearing and behave yourself."

"You can't tell me what to do," she said.

"If you don't be good, I'm going to punch you," I said. "Besides, they won't give you any strawberry ice cream."

So she washed, and when she got done I snatched up the washcloth and went over the parts she'd missed. She was pretty dirty. There were stains all over her jeans—dirt stains from lying in the woods, ketchup stains from the hot dogs, and a whole lot of other stains I couldn't identify, they were so old. I looked down at my own jeans; they weren't much better. I decided that I'd wash all our clothes in the bathtub or something before we went to bed, so they'd be dry in the morning.

We went into the dining room. It was something, all right—just the way Gussie always described it. The table was set with a white cloth and sparkling glasses and silverware; and, in the middle, a bowl of fresh flowers. There was a big, old wooden sideboard against one wall with dishes and bottles of wine on it, and on the walls there hung more old-fashioned people. I didn't know that anyone could have so many ancestors.

But the white tablecloth worried me, for I knew that within two minutes it would be six different colors where Ooma was sitting. "Maybe we ought to put a newspaper under Ooma's plate."

Our grandmother laughed. "She's as bad as all that?"

"She likes to eat with her fingers," I said.

"Well, we won't worry about it tonight, Fergy," our grandmother said.

We sat down, and in a minute the maid came out of the kitchen carrying a plate with a lot of slices of beef on it. I figured she would put it down on the table so our grandmother could serve it. But she didn't. She went and stood by our grandmother, and our grandmother helped herself to a slice of beef with a big serving fork. So that was the idea. Then she went around to Ooma and stood there.

I said, "You're supposed to serve yourself, Ooma."

"Oh," she said. She reached up with her hand and snatched a slice of beef off the plate. And then, as the maid started to move away, she snatched another one. "I love this kind of meat," she said.

I went red as a tomato and hot as fire. She was bound to get us thrown out of there before dinner was over. "She's really okay," I said. "She doesn't know better. Maybe I can teach her."

"Don't worry about it, Fergy," our grandfather said. "We don't mind."

But I *did* worry about it, for I could see that it was going to be mighty tough to teach Ooma their ways. She wasn't used to that style at all. Then the maid came around to me, and I picked up the fork and caught hold of a piece of meat and managed to get it onto my plate without dropping it on the floor.

Next, the maid brought in the boiled potatoes. When she came around to Ooma I said, "Use a spoon, not your fingers."

Ooma gave me a look, but she picked up the spoon out of the serving dish and took a jab into it. A potato hopped out and landed on the floor. I went red. "See what you made me do," she said. She slid out of her chair, picked up the potato, and put it back into the bowl. Then she kneeled up in her chair and took a couple of potatoes out of the bowl with her fingers. "I love these kind of potatoes, too."

I looked at our grandparents. They were smiling. "Are you sure you can eat all that, Ooma?" our grandmother said.

"Sure I can. You should see how much I can eat."

Our grandfather burst out laughing. "I'll bet you can," he said.

"What's so damn funny?" she said. "I can eat a hell of a lot."

Next, the maid came out with a bowl of peas with butter melting on them. "She doesn't want any," I said. "Peas make her break out."

"That's a damn lie, Fergy. I love peas."

"Sheila, I think you'd better help Ooma to the peas," our grandmother said.

That was a big relief. I managed to help myself without spilling more than a couple on the table. Ooma was already digging in, hanging onto the meat with one hand while she sawed at it with the knife, splashing stuff off her plate, eating the potatoes with her fingers, so that in five minutes there was food scattered all around her. Some of her peas were halfway across the table to me. She didn't mind. She just picked the stuff off the tablecloth and ate it as she went along. I tried not to watch. Besides, I wasn't so hot at table manners myself and had to keep watching our grandparents out of the corners of my eyes to see how they cut their meat and what they did with their forks and knives when they picked up their glasses of water. It took a lot of concentration, and every time they asked me a question I had to stop eating, because I couldn't answer questions and watch my table manners at the same time. So I didn't get much of a chance to worry about Ooma; and by the time we were finished with dinner, her place looked like a map, it had so many different colors on it.

After dinner, our grandmother took Ooma upstairs to give her a bubble bath. Ooma had never heard of bubble baths, and she was willing to try one. My grandfather took me back to the living room so we could talk and he could drink his coffee. What sort of plans did I have for the future?

I didn't want to come right out and say that I wanted to live with them. That was bound to sound like I was trying to get myself rich out of them. So I just said that I wanted, somehow, to go to a regular school and join the Boy Scouts and play trumpet or something in a school band and be on some kind of a team.

"What about Ooma?" he said.

"She only came because I made her come," I said. "But she shouldn't stay with Gussie and J. P. anymore. She's already got a habit of stealing things, and she's bound to get into real trouble sooner or later. The trouble is, she doesn't like being regular. She likes being dirty and stealing and living in vans."

"And you say J. P. stole that motor home? Do they do that sort of thing often?"

"No, nothing so big, usually. At least as far as I know. All they ever stole before was food out of supermarkets, or maybe a couple of cans of oil from a gas station or something."

He sat there stirring his coffee and staring down into it. "They're bound to get into serious difficulties sooner or later," he said. "It's not a good situation, Fergy, and you're right to want to get out of it. And get Ooma out of it, too."

"The only thing is, it may be too late for Ooma to change."

He sipped at his coffee. "What made you change? How did that come about?"

I frowned, thinking about it. "I guess I always was this way. I never liked being dirty or stealing or any of that, right from when I was little, back on the old commune. Even then I liked going to school and learning things. They had a kind of weird school on that place one winter when they didn't have anything interesting to do, and I liked going to that, even though it was only wildflowers and sex education.''

He didn't say anything for a minute, but rubbed his hand on his chin. Then he said, ''How do you intend to do any of this—go to school and join the Boy Scouts and so forth?''

There wasn't any way around it now. I had to answer straight out. ''I—I hoped maybe we could come and live with you.''

He sat there rubbing his chin and thinking. Finally he said, ''Fergy, you have to understand that legally you belong to Gussie and J. P., and there's no way we can keep you here if they want you back.''

I didn't know if that meant he might let us stay or was thinking of excuses for sending us back. ''Maybe they won't find out where we are.''

He shook his head. ''Sooner or later they'll find out. We have to expect that.''

I still wasn't sure which way he was deciding. ''Maybe it'll take a while,'' I said. ''Maybe by that time I'll be old enough to decide for myself.''

''Perhaps,'' he said. ''But I wouldn't count on it. They're surely going to be looking for the two of you. In time, it'll occur to them that you might have come here.''

What could I say to talk him into it? There must be something I could say. I stared down at the carpet, trying to think of something. ''Maybe J. P. wouldn't want to come here to get us.''

''He'll come, once he knows,'' he said.

I knew that was right. I couldn't think of anything more to say.

''Fergy, don't misunderstand me,'' he said. ''We're not going to turn you away. We'll be very happy to have you stay here for the time being, anyway. Let's just see how it works out."

Just then, Ooma came downstairs with our grandmother. She was clean and her hair was braided and she was wearing a cute little pink dress. I was amazed at how pretty she looked. "Look, Fergy," she said. "Gussie's dress when she was my age." She was pleased as could be with herself. Then we went out onto the porch and ate strawberry ice cream in ginger ale, watching the people go along the sidewalk in the streetlight. Ooma got strawberry ice cream all over the pink dress, which I guess is why our grandmother picked that color. But I didn't care, because I was mighty happy.

THIRTEEN

SO WE STARTED to live with them. They had lots of space, and we each had our own room. It made Ooma nervous sleeping in a room all by herself; she'd spent most of her life sleeping in the back of a van with a bunch of people lying all over each other, and she wasn't used to being alone. At first, she would come into my room as soon as I shut my light off and crawl into bed with me. I let her a couple of times, but then I told her she couldn't. I loved having a room of my own. I could hardly get over the idea of it. I had a bureau and a bookcase full of books and a view out the window at the beautiful back garden. Sometimes I would just look around at all the things and say under my breath, "It's mine, it's all mine." It surprised me every time I thought about it.

They bought us a whole lot of clothes, too, stuff I'd never had before, like a jacket and a necktie and real shoes instead of sneakers. I got Grandfather to show me how to tie the necktie, and I stood in front of the mirror practicing and practicing until I got it. Sometimes I would get all dressed up in the tie and jacket and the regular shoes and just stand there and look at myself in the mirror. I was kind of ashamed of myself for being proud when I did that. I felt guilty for being rich and having all kinds of wonderful things, when there were so many poor people in the world who had practically nothing at all. But I couldn't help myself. I liked having things and being able to dress up and all; and I decided it would be okay to be rich, if I felt guilty about it sometimes.

They didn't send us to a regular school. Grandfather said we were too far behind for that. So he got tutors to teach us at home. There were three or four of them, and they came on different days and taught us arithmetic and spelling and history and so forth. Grandfather said we'd catch up a whole lot faster that way. When we were caught up, he would send us to private schools, and at last I would have a jacket with an emblem on it and play on some team.

But it didn't take me more than a week to realize that Ooma wasn't suited to it at all. She liked having Grandmother make a fuss over her and give her bubble baths, and take her shopping for clothes and then for sodas at some fancy place afterward. She liked having horseback lessons, and she liked being able to run around in the garden and lie in the grass and smell the flowers. But she didn't like the rest of it very much. She didn't like having to eat in that big dining room and be polite; she was used to eating whenever she felt like it and grabbing whatever she wanted. She didn't like being tutored at all. She spent the whole time her tutors were there twisting and turning in her seat, staring out the window and chewing on the eraser of her pencil. The tutors were always bawling her out for something. She didn't like that, either, because she wasn't used to being bawled out. She didn't like hanging up her clothes and cutting her fingernails and getting her hair shampooed all the time.

The trouble was that our grandparents had a lot of rules. They didn't think they had a lot of rules, but they did. They were always saying that they'd been too hard on Gussie, that they shouldn't have been so strict with her and made her take lessons in everything and learn how to serve tea and be polite. They'd learned their lesson, they said, and they'd never do it that way again. But they still had an awful lot of rules. I guess that if you're used to a hundred rules, fifty doesn't seem like very much. But Ooma'd been used to about two rules, and any more than that seemed like too many.

Me, I liked having the rules. I liked the idea of everything being set and organized for a change. I liked knowing that if I listened to what the tutors said and studied what they told me to study, I would catch up and stop being dumb. I liked knowing when I was supposed to get up in the morning and what time lunch was. I liked knowing that if I finally went to a private school and got to be friendly with the other kids, and one of them asked me over to dinner, I'd know all the right table manners and how to serve myself from the maid, if they had one.

But not Ooma—she didn't like having any rules at all. By the end of the first week we were there, she was being low and quiet. It wasn't like her to be low and quiet, and I knew there was bound to be an explosion if I didn't do something. For I knew that if Ooma went back to Gussie and J. P., they'd know where I was and come after me, too. I couldn't let that happen; I had to keep her from deciding to go back. So one night, when we were supposed to be doing our homework, I went into her room to talk to her.

She was lying on her bed looking at a magazine— she still couldn't read enough to read a book. I sat down in her chair. "Ooma, you ought to try not to be so grumpy. You don't realize how lucky you are."

"I want to get the hell out of here."

"Give it a little more chance. Once you get used to it, you'll probably like it."

"I'll never get used to this damn place. You made me come here. I wish we didn't come."

"If you go back to live with Gussie and J. P., you're bound to get into big trouble sooner or later."

"Why would I?"

"What about that time in New York you stole all that money?"

"The system is always ripping us off." She heaved the magazine across the room. "We have a right to rip them off."

"Just because J. P. says that doesn't mean you have to believe it."

"Why shouldn't I believe it if I want to?" she said. "It's right, isn't it?"

"I don't think it's right," I said.

"Well, I do," she said. "I just want to get the hell out of this damn place. Why did you make me come here, anyway?"

I could see that there wasn't any point in arguing with her. She wasn't in a mood to listen to anything I said. So I dropped it; but I knew there was going to be an explosion, and it came three or four days later.

That afternoon, I was up in my room writing an essay on the planets when I heard Grandmother come upstairs and go into Ooma's room. In a minute she opened my door and put her head in. "Where's Ooma, Fergy? The reading teacher is here."

"I don't know," I said. "Isn't she in her room?"

"No, she's not."

"Maybe she's in the bathroom," I said.

"I looked in there," she said.

I began to get the feeling that Ooma was up to something. I figured I'd better find her myself before they did. "I'll go look for her," I said. I went into Ooma's room. There was a good chance that she'd hidden when she'd heard Grandmother coming. I looked under her bed and in her closet, but she wasn't there. I checked the bathroom again, in case she'd hidden in the shower, but she wasn't there, either. I went back into her room to see if all her clothes were still there. I didn't think she'd take off on her own—that would have been too scary for her. But I checked, anyway, and her clothes were still there.

I was just about to go downstairs when, through the window, I saw something move out in the garden. I went downstairs and out back through the glass doors in the living room. There was a birdbath in the middle of the lawn and, beyond that, flower beds. I couldn't see Ooma. I crossed the lawn to the other side, and then I saw her.

She was lying flat on her back in the middle of a flower bed. The flowers all around her were broken and flattened. She had her shirt off, and she was rubbing her chest with a handful of dirt and flowers mixed together.

"Ooma, are you crazy?" I said.

"I'm sick of this crappy place," she shouted. "I can't stand it anymore. I want to go back to Gussie and J. P."

"Ooma, get out of there," I said. "Grandmother's going to have a fit when she sees what you're doing."

"I don't give a damn," she said. "I don't care what she thinks."

I started to jump into the flower bed to haul her out of it, when I realized that Grandmother and Grandfather were coming across the lawn toward us. I grabbed her arm, jerked her to her feet, and dragged her out of the bed onto the lawn. There were dirt and bits of flowers all over her chest, and on her face, too. She swung with her fist to slug me, but I ducked back into the garden and picked up her shirt. Then our grandparents were there.

"What is this, Ooma?" Grandmother said. "What have you been doing?"

"I'm sick of this damn place," she shouted. "I'm

sick of all these damn rules. I want to go back to Gussie and J. P.''

Our grandparents looked at each other. Then Grandfather said, ''All right, Ooma, let's go inside and talk about it.''

''I don't want to talk about it,'' she shouted. ''I just want to go home.''

''But, Ooma,'' Grandmother said, ''we don't know where your parents are.''

''I'll find them,'' she shouted.

Grandfather put his arm around her shoulder. ''All right, calm down. We'll see what we can do about it.'' He started walking her toward the house, and Grandmother and I followed along behind them. I was feeling rotten about what might happen to me.

Grandmother gave Ooma some ice cream and got her calmed down, and finally she was willing to have a bubble bath and put on clean clothes. So she and Grandmother went upstairs, and Grandfather and I sat in the living room.

''Do you have any idea where they are, Fergy?'' he said.

''Because of having the stolen motor home, they're trying to stay out in the country away from cities.''

''You don't have any better idea than that?''

''No,'' I said. ''They were out in Arkansas when we ran away, and they might be around there someplace. But they're in the habit of traveling around a lot, because you can't sell that honey and stuff to the same people all the time.''

He nodded. ''Fergy, you understand that we can't keep Ooma here if she's going to be miserable all the time.''

''Yes,'' I said. He was right, but it didn't make me feel any better.

''I've been watching her the past few days, and I

125

could see she'd lost her spark. She was like a wild animal in a trap. Did you notice?"

"Yes," I said. "I was hoping she'd get over it."

"We thought that in time she'd get used to things here, but it doesn't seem so. I'm afraid it's going to take a long time to civilize her. It's a shame. She's intelligent and she's pretty when she takes care of herself, but she just doesn't seem to care for any of that."

"Maybe she will when she's older."

"It may be too late then. I don't know. You never can tell how these things will work out." He took off his glasses and stared at the ceiling. "How? How are we going to find them?"

"Grandfather, if they take her they'll take me, too."

He put his glasses back on and looked at me. "They'll try to, Fergy. I know that. It's the risk we have to take. We can't keep Ooma here if she's as miserable as she's been."

"Maybe if we gave her a little more time."

He nodded. "It's worth a try."

So they had a talk with Ooma and got her to agree to stick it out a little longer and see if she got more used to their ways. A week went by. I worked as hard as I could on my studies, because I knew it might be my last chance to catch up. When I got a chance I tried to talk Ooma into staying. "You'll be able to go to a fancy school and meet a lot of rich kids and marry a rich guy when you grow up."

"I hate rich guys," she said. "They're bourgeois."

"Don't you like new clothes and being pretty instead of looking like a pig all the time?"

"What's wrong with old clothes?" she said. "I like them."

"If you go back to the motor home you won't get all this good stuff to eat—ice cream and roast beef and cake."

"I don't care," she said. "I want to go back to Gussie and J. P."

Finally, I realized that I couldn't talk her out of it, and I stopped trying. And then one morning I went up to her room to tell her that her reading tutor was there. She wasn't there, and I was about to knock on the bathroom door to see if she was there, when I heard a radio playing softly somewhere in the room. That surprised me, because she didn't have a radio. I cocked my head to listen, and in a couple of seconds I determined that it was coming from the bed. I jumped over there and snatched up the pillow. And sure enough, there lay a little transistor radio.

I picked it up, and just then Ooma came back into the room, tucking her shirt into her skirt. "Where did you get this?" I said.

"Grandmother gave it to me," she said.

"You're a big liar," I said. "You stole it."

"None of your damn business," she said. She grabbed at it, but I snatched my hand back in time.

"Who did you steal it from?"

"None of your business," she said, and grabbed for it again.

I figured I knew. Grandmother and Grandfather weren't much interested in listening to the radio. If they wanted to hear a concert or something, they usually put records on the big stereo in the den. But the maids listened while they worked. "You stole this from one of the maids, didn't you? From Sheila."

All she said was, "Give it back to me," and made another grab for it, so I knew I was right. I stuck it in my pocket and ducked around her out of the room. I went downstairs to give it back to Sheila, feeling sick, for I knew that if Ooma was starting to steal again, she would have to go back to Gussie and J. P. I didn't want to tell Grandfather, but I had to, and I did.

He nodded. "It isn't the stealing," he said. "The money's not important. But it's a sign that she's unhappy, Fergy. That kind of thing always is."

"Then why did she steal all the time when we lived in the van? She was supposed to be happy living that way."

Grandfather nodded. "I imagine that she wasn't quite as happy about all of that as she seemed. Right now, she's homesick and she misses her mother, which would be normal in a child her age. But when you get down to it, that was a fairly insecure life you were all living. I mean, never knowing if you'd have a good dinner, and always worried about being run out of someplace by the police. Most children like to know that there'll be food on the table and a roof over their heads the next day."

I could agree with that, all right. I never liked living that way myself, and I guess maybe that down inside, Ooma didn't like it as much as she thought she did. But there was no way around it—she was determined to go back to J. P. and Gussie, and we had to let her do it.

"I'm not going back with them," I said. "I'll run away again."

"Let's cross that bridge when we get to it, Fergy," Grandfather said.

The question now was how to find the motor home. The easiest thing would have been to call the police and put them on the lookout for it. But we didn't dare do that, for the police were bound to discover that the motor home had been stolen, and then J. P. and Gussie and the rest would be in serious trouble. So Grandfather hired a private detective to look for them, a man who specialized in finding missing persons. He told Grandfather that there was a good chance of finding them.

"It seems like a needle in a haystack looking for somebody in a country as big as the United States, but people leave trails. They're out in public with that little business of theirs. People are going to remember them. I'll have one of my associates who operates out of the Memphis area start driving around to shopping malls and asking questions. We know that they tend to work out of suburban malls, and if they're still in that area, he's bound to find somebody who remembers them. Once we catch hold of one end of a string, it's relatively easy to follow it out.''

After that Grandfather said that Ooma didn't have to study anymore if she didn't want to or have horseback-riding lessons, either. And she could wear old clothes, too; but she would have to keep herself clean and eat with the rest of us and at least try to use good table manners.

The whole thing kind of surprised Ooma. She wanted to go back to Gussie and J. P.—that was clear enough. But suddenly being allowed to sit around all day and look at magazines or watch TV, she felt sort of out of things. Sometimes when one of my tutors came she would hang around in the den where he was teaching me, curled up in a big chair, sucking her thumb. Or when they took me in to the Boston Symphony one Sunday to expose me to good music, she said she wanted to go.

"You'd just be bored, Ooma," Grandmother said. "Besides, you'd have to dress properly, and you know you don't like to do that."

She looked at me in my shirt and tie and jacket and shoes that I'd shined up so they gleamed. "I wouldn't mind dressing up this time," she said, kind of sad.

"No, you'd just be bored," Grandmother said. I knew Grandmother was trying to get Ooma to see what she would be missing when she went back to Gussie and J. P. I felt sorry for her, but she'd asked for it.

So a week went by, and another one, and I was beginning to get up hopes that the missing persons detective wasn't as smart as he thought he was and would never find them, when one night as we were eating dinner the phone rang. The maid answered, and in a minute she came into the dining room. "Excuse me, Mr. Hamilton. It's a woman who says she's your daughter."

"Does that mean Gussie?" Ooma said. Her eyes began to shine.

"Yes," Grandfather said. He looked at me and Grandmother, and then he got up and went down the hall to his den to answer the phone.

Grandmother turned her head to stare out into the garden. "Fifteen years," she said. "It's been fifteen years."

Ooma jumped out of her seat. "Where is she? Can I go see her?"

"We don't know where she is yet, Ooma. We have to wait until Grandfather finishes talking to her. Now sit down and finish your dinner."

But Ooma couldn't sit still. She kept jumping off her chair and running down the hall toward the den to see if Grandfather had finished talking. I would get her and bring her back, and about two minutes later she would jump down and race off again.

I felt pretty bad. In a while—a few days, maybe even a few hours—they would drive up in the motor home and take me back, and I'd be living with them again, playing guitar in shopping malls, living on hot dogs and peanut-butter sandwiches, wearing old clothes, taking showers in YMCAs and public bathhouses, and getting dumb all over again. How I wished that that guy had never found them. Oh, how I wished they'd forgotten about us altogether.

Then Grandfather came back into the dining room. He looked at Grandmother. "It wasn't that detective who found them," he said.

She looked surprised. "Not the detective?"

"No," he said. He sat down at the table and put his napkin in his lap to go on eating. He looked mighty grim. "They're all in jail. They got caught for stealing the motor home. They're being held for ten thousand dollars bail. Augusta called to ask us for the bail money."

Grandmother pulled her lips tight together. Then she said, "Did you tell her that the children are here?"

"I had to," Grandfather said, picking up his fork. "She said they wouldn't have been arrested, but she was so worried about the children that she went to the police about it. She was afraid they had been kidnapped, or worse."

FOURTEEN

THE WHOLE THING made me feel terrible. I'd got my own mom and dad put in jail. I had trouble going to sleep that night for thinking about it. I tossed and turned, wishing that somehow I had bothered to figure out a way of letting Gussie know we were okay. If only I had done that, they wouldn't have got put in jail. I could have told her we'd found Mr. and Mrs. Clappers and gone to live with them. She'd have believed that and wouldn't have worried so much. Or I could have told her we'd got put in a home someplace, but wanted to stay there and weren't going to tell her where it was. I could have thought of something, and I could have figured out a way to get a message to her. But I hadn't; I'd been too worried all along about saving myself and hadn't given Gussie any thought, and now she was in jail.

For it was clear enough that it was Gussie who'd gone to the police. She'd told Grandfather so. J. P. hadn't wanted to take the chance; they'd find us themselves, he said. But it was too much of a worry for Gussie, so she took the chance and went to the police.

The next morning at breakfast I still felt terrible about it. I sat there with my poached egg in front of me, stabbing at it but not eating it, feeling rotten. Grandfather said, "Fergy, there's no point in borrowing trouble. We don't know what'll happen until they come. Perhaps we can work something out."

"It isn't that, Grandfather," I said. "I'm worried because it's all my fault. If I'd sent them a note saying we were okay, they wouldn't have got into trouble."

"How on earth did you expect to send them a note, Fergy?" Grandmother said.

"I could have figured out some way."

"Fergy, they didn't get into trouble because of you," Grandfather said. "They got into trouble because they stole that motor home."

That was so; I could see that. "Well, even so, I should have sent them a note."

"Fergy, you blame yourself too much," Grandmother said. But I didn't think I did.

They had got caught out in Kansas and were in some jail there. Grandfather arranged for the bail money to be sent out there. They would be allowed to go free until the trial came. "The bail money is to make sure they come back for the trial," Grandfather said. "If they decide to disappear, we lose the money."

That was pretty worrisome, for it sounded likely to me that J. P. and the Wiz would say it was just another example of the system ripping them off. Grandfather was part of the system and hadn't earned all of his money but inherited it, and so they were just as entitled to it as he was. They'd come and get us and not go back for the trial, but just take off for someplace. After that, we'd be on the run from the police the whole time.

So Grandfather sent the money, and we waited for a day, and then another and another. Finally, on the fourth day, around three o'clock in the afternoon when I was in my room doing my arithmetic homework, I heard the front doorbell ring, and Ooma shouting and racing down the front hall, and I knew it was them.

I didn't want to see them. I wanted to hide up there in my room until they went away. I heard Grandfather's voice, and then J. P. saying loudly, "Where have you got Fergy?'' Then Gussie said something soft, and I knew I would have to go down there and see them.

I went down the stairs to the front hall. The front door was wide open, and they were all standing there, sort of half in the house and half out on the porch— Gussie and J. P. and Grandmother and Grandfather and Ooma. Ooma had her arms around Gussie's waist and her head resting on Gussie's side, and Gussie had her arm around Ooma's shoulder.

They all stopped talking and looked at me. "Fergy,'' J. P. shouted. "What the hell did you think you were doing pulling a stunt like that? Can't you see what a mess you've got us in?''

I looked at him. "I don't want to go back with you,'' I said. "Ooma can go if she wants, but I'm not going.''

"Oh, yes you are, Fergy,'' J. P. said. "You're going to do what you're told. You've got a lot to make up for to the rest of us.''

Grandfather said, "We don't have to stand here in the hall. Let's go in and sit down and talk about it calmly.''

"No, thanks,'' J. P. said. "I don't want anything from you. I came to collect my kids and go. Fergy, go get in the van. I don't want to be in this house a minute longer than I have to.''

Gussie unwrapped Ooma's arms from her, came over to me, and gave me a hug. I didn't hug her back, but stood stiff with my arms straight down my sides and looked past her. "It's all right, Fergy,'' she said. "It wasn't your fault.''

"Don't put ideas in his head, Gussie,'' J. P. said. "He's already too big for his pants.''

"I'm not going back with you,'' I said.

"Mr. Wheeler,'' Grandfather said, "Fergy's done so well here. He's getting caught up in his studies, and I think by fall he may be ready for school. I'm quite willing to stand the expense of—''

"I'll bet you are," J. P. said. "You'll spend anything you have in order to poison his mind with your dirty ideas. No, thanks, Hamilton. They're going with me." He grabbed Ooma by her shoulder. "Go on out to the van, Ooma."

She started to go, but then Gussie said, "Just a minute, Ooma. J. P., I'm going to stay here for a couple of days. I haven't been here for fifteen years. I want a chance to talk to my mother and father a little bit."

"Gussie, I told you before I don't want you doing that," J. P. said loudly. "We're all going now. Right now. Ooma, Fergy, go out and get in the van."

"No, J. P. I want them to stay here with me for a couple of days."

J. P. grabbed Ooma's shoulder and gave her a push toward the door. "Out, Ooma. I'm not going to stand for any back talk from any of you." He jerked his head toward the street. "Out in the van, all of you."

"Mr. Wheeler," Grandfather said, "take your hand off that child or I'll have the police on you in five minutes."

J. P. stared at Grandfather. "Don't you try to pull anything on me, Hamilton."

"I'm warning you, Mr. Wheeler, I'll have the police on you. The children's mother wants them with her. If you think that isn't sufficient, I advise you to get a lawyer and go to court. Now, get off my property, before I have you arrested."

"I'm taking my kids," J. P. said. He snatched Ooma off the ground and swung around to head off the porch to the street. But Ooma shrieked, "Let me go, J. P. I want to stay with Gussie." She made a grab for his hair and started pulling.

"Why, you little brat," he shouted. He pulled her hand loose from his hair and dropped her onto the ground. Gussie ran over to Ooma, picked her up, and darted back into the house with her. "She's staying with me for a couple of days, J. P."

J. P. stood there glaring around. "You can bet I'm going to see a lawyer," he said. "You can't take a man's kids away from him."

"It'll only be a couple of days," Gussie said. "Come back in a couple of days."

Nobody said anything. J. P. looked around at us all. "Please get off my property, Mr. Wheeler," Grandfather said. J. P. slammed the door with a big bang.

Well, I didn't know what was going on, or what to think. Gussie and J. P. had had some kind of big fight, that was clear enough. What was it about? I wanted to get Gussie aside and ask her, but I didn't have a chance. First Ooma wanted her to go upstairs with her and show her about having a bubble bath, and then she and Grandfather and Grandmother went into the living room to talk. They talked all afternoon. Around five o'clock Grandfather and Gussie went out somewhere in the car. Ooma and I had dinner with Grandmother. I asked her some questions, but all she would say was, "I think we'll leave it to your mother to explain it all." So Ooma and I went to bed, and when we got up in the morning, Gussie and Grandmother and Grandfather were already in the living room drinking coffee and talking some more. I wasn't surprised that they were talking so much. They hadn't seen each other for fifteen years. They had an awful lot to catch up on.

Finally, they told Ooma and me to come in. We sat on the sofa side by side, and Gussie sat on the other sofa with Grandmother, and Grandfather sat in his big chair. Gussie said, "Ooma, do you really want to go back and live in the van again?"

"We don't have to live in the van," Ooma said. "We can live in the motor home."

Gussie shook her head. "We had to give the motor home back."

"I thought J. P. said we had a right to it."

"J. P. was wrong about that. We had to give it back."

"Oh," Ooma said. "Maybe we could swipe another one."

Gussie frowned. "Ooma, we've all got to stop stealing," she said. "We got caught stealing the motor home, and we all may have to go to jail."

"You might go to jail?"

"Yes," Gussie said.

Ooma put her thumb in her mouth, and in a little bit I could see the tears start to come out of her eyes. I felt like crying myself; the idea of your own mother going to jail was pretty terrible. "It's all my fault," I said. "It wouldn't have happened if I hadn't made Ooma run away."

Gussie shook her head. "It isn't your fault, Fergy. It's my fault. I should have left J. P. the minute he took the motor home. In fact, I've been thinking about taking you away with me for some time. I could see what was happening to Ooma. But I didn't have a way of making a living. I didn't know how we would live. Then J. P. stole the motor home and I knew I would have to do something. It's been terrible the last few weeks, riding around in that thing and being scared to death every time we passed a police car. And then you kids disappeared, and after that I knew I couldn't go on living like that any longer. What use were J. P.'s big ideas if I'd lost my kids on account of them? So I decided to go to the police. J. P. told me not to do it. He said you two hadn't been kidnapped; he'd noticed how moody Fergy had been and that it was clear that you'd run away. We'd find you ourselves. But I didn't want to take a chance, so I went to the police and, of course, they wanted the license number of the motor home. They checked it out and found out it'd been stolen. We were camped out in some woods, and they came and arrested us.''

Ooma took her thumb out of her mouth. "What did they do with the motor home?" she said.

"The insurance company took it," she said. "They'd already paid the Clapperses for another one, so it belonged to them."

"Did you see Mr. and Mrs. Clappers?" Ooma said.

"No," Gussie said. "I don't think they would have wanted to see us very much."

That made me feel sad, and I decided someday I would try to find out their address and write them a letter saying I was sorry about what had happened. But I didn't say anything about that. Instead, I said, "But, Gussie, that farmer told you he'd just given us a ride. You must have known we weren't kidnapped."

Gussie shrugged. "In a way, that made it worse. We knew you were wandering around out there somewhere and didn't know what kind of people you might run into. J. P. said we'd find you ourselves, but I didn't want to take a chance."

Nobody said anything. Then Ooma said, "Are you really going to jail, Gussie?"

"I might have to," she said. "Your grandfather took me around to see his lawyer yesterday evening, and he said he thought perhaps he could arrange for me to get a suspended sentence, but I would have to tell the whole truth about everything. J. P. and the Wiz and Trotsky would be found guilty."

"Are you going to do it?" I said.

"Fergy, it's either that or spend the rest of my life running away. I'd rather face up to it now and have it over with than worry about the police forever. I was against stealing the motor home, and I didn't help them

138

take it. But, still, I'm an accomplice: I should have taken you two right then and left.''

"J. P. has to go to jail, too?" Ooma said.

Gussie came over and sat down between us and put her arms around both of us. "No, he won't, Ooma. Not right now, anyway. He and the Wiz and Trotsky won't go back to stand trial. They'll take off for somewhere in the van, and it'll probably be a long time before they catch them. That's why I couldn't let him take you with him. How would I ever find you again if I went back to Kansas and stood trial and you were on the run with him?''

My mouth dropped open. "You mean, we're all going to stay here?" I said.

"Yes, I think we will for a while," she said. "First, I have to go back to Kansas and see if the judge will give me a suspended sentence for telling them the whole story. Then, I have to see about finishing my education myself and getting a job.''

"But won't J. P. come after us?" I said.

"He won't dare, Fergy," Grandfather said. "He won't dare take the case to court, because it's bound to come out that he's wanted for car theft in Kansas. Besides, no judge in his right mind is going to send children off to live with their father in a van, when they have a good home with their mother. And J. P. won't dare come and try to scoop you up. He knows we'd have the police on him in five minutes, and he wouldn't stand a chance of getting out of Cambridge, much less Massachusetts, before they caught him.''

Now I began to cry, because it was going to work out in the end. I sat there crying, feeling stupid. Then Ooma put her arms around my neck. "Don't cry, Fergy," she said. "I'll try to eat right and stuff, and I won't steal anymore. Mostly.''

JAMES LINCOLN COLLIER is a musician and editor as well as the award-winning author of many books for young people. His novels include the Newbery Honor Book *My Brother Sam Is Dead* (with his brother Christopher Collier), *Planet Out of the Past,* and *The Teddy Bear Habit.* His books on jazz include *Inside Jazz, The Great Jazz Artists,* and *Louis Armstrong.* He lives in New York City.